RED WATER

SHADOWS OF CAMELOT CROSSING

LISA COURTAWAY

LISA COURTAWAY

RED WATER

A HAUNTING IN STILLWATER

RED WATER

A HAUNTING IN STILLWATER

Some secrets insist on coming to light...

Moving is never easy, especially during a pandemic. But the Weizak family plans to make the best of their transition to Camelot Crossing in the sleepy college town of Stillwater, Oklahoma.

Sure, their quirky new Tudor home is enormous and strangely designed, more like a curious castle than a cozy shelter. But it shouldn't be that hard to settle in and feel safe.

If only the long vacant house...and its creepy nightly visitor...would cooperate.

What starts with an odd message from their Alexa and mysterious footsteps in the hallway soon evolves into a bizarre haunting that has the entire Weizak family convinced their home is slowly turning against them. Ignoring the unexplained happenings only seems to make things worse.

The house—or its unseen inhabitant—will not rest any longer. No, it will go to any lengths necessary to expose the horrible event that happened decades earlier on its lonely, rain-soaked grounds. But will it drive the Weizaks away before it's too late?

A NEW OLD-FASHIONED GHOST STORY SET IN A SMALL COLLEGE TOWN... RED WATER - SHADOWS OF CAMELOT CROSSING WILL KEEP YOU GUESSING UNTIL THE VERY END.

Editing and Formatting by Three Point Author Services
www.threepointauthorservices.com

Cover Design by Miblart
www.miblart.com

*Dedicated to the town of Stillwater, and in loving memory of
Sam Childers, Sr. and C. Kirk.*

Her world changed in a flash
She could no longer grow
She was ageless and wandering in a foreign space
Watching life move on
Over time she learned to find her voice again
She would use that voice to make sure her story was told

ONE

The house leered at them, uninviting under the thick morning clouds. *House* was too basic a word to describe the massive Tudor. It could legitimately be called a mansion. The Weizaks weren't the mansion type.

The heavy air added to the menacing spirit of the expansive grounds as the family of four exited their SUV to take in their new "forever home." A blanket of dew, remnants of a chilly night, clung to everything and was trapped by the canopy of trees, creating an oppressive atmosphere as the temperature rose higher with each passing minute. Tiny buds of color could be glimpsed dotting the gray forest and sprouting in the brown grass, new life rushing forward to cast out winter's deadening chill.

They all had different opinions regarding the move. Dad, for reasons only a father could dream up, had always longed to live in a quiet, small town, one that still had a forward-thinking sensibility. A college town like rural Stillwater, Oklahoma would be perfect. Home of the OSU Cowboys, Pistol Pete, and numerous quaint traditions, Stillwater had one foot in the past while the other was running toward the future. Saturday tailgating and homecoming parades in the fall—Go, team! This from a man who was far more interested in tech stocks than any team sports, but who only ever strove to make his entire family happy.

Their experience in Tempe, home of the ASU Sun Devils, hadn't come near the college-town life he had mapped out in budget charts, investment reports, and his dream of the ideal life. Arizona hadn't hit the mark. Just before the twins started kindergarten, the family left the crowded city and searing heat, seeking a slower pace in Tulsa, Oklahoma. Dad's career required the family be uprooted a few times as he sought a balance of work and home life that suited him and his family. The result was a maddening few years in which multiple moves took them from Oklahoma, to Utah, back to Oklahoma and then to Colorado. Dad's fervent wish was that Stillwater would strike the perfect chord, and they could remain and thrive in the tranquil town.

Mom was overjoyed to be leaving the mid-century modern house that never quite worked for them behind in Colorado. Like the previous localities the Weizaks had called home over the years, the Centennial State never tooted Mom's horn. It seemed she didn't fit in anywhere besides her home state of Oklahoma, because they always bounced back to her birthplace. It was as if a magnet twitched inside her soul, always drawing her to return to the humid summers and unpredictable springs. While she never dreamed she'd be back in the town of her alma mater, she had loved her time in Stillwater during her college days, and anything had to be better than Colorado. She never denied the beauty of the mountains; she just hated snow. Tornado Alley did experience the occasional villainous winter storm, but she appreciated the state's tendency to shut down, allowing her to admire the beauty from the safety and comfort of home. Snow days were an anomaly in Colorado. She missed the surprise awakenings, when work and school were put on hold, and complained loudly as she white-knuckled her way to those obligations on the snow-packed Colorado roads in the frigid cold.

Holden could only be pulled away from his Alienware by his iPhone, and in turn could be torn from his iPhone only when absolutely required. So the teen wasn't too bummed by the move. He acted perturbed because garnering sympathy via guilt trips had proven very lucrative over the years, especially when big nuisances were involved, like moving ... again. He had mastered the art of profiting from parental penitence. The time and energy involved in moving was brutal, no doubt, but he had never bonded with any new friends in the other towns they had lived. However, he had remained tight with the group he attended elementary school with during the family's longest stint in Tulsa. (Yes, there were two moves to Tulsa. The second was after a disagreeable, but thankfully brief, call-it-a-layover in Salt Lake City, which sent them fleeing back to Tulsa in a matter of months.)

For Holden, every member of his Tulsa crew was never further than a click away. Technology allowed him to hang with his true friends anytime, from any place. And the Weizaks' new house, while beyond weird, had the perfect setup for his gaming gear. At least it appeared to, in the well-lit, fish-eye lens pictures of the real estate listing. He knew a lot about housing markets and buying decisions by osmosis, it seemed. What a useless mind-suck for a teen.

Hazel, Holden's younger sister—by four minutes—was the most distraught at yet another upheaval. She definitely had the most to lose. Like her best friend in the whole world, Miren Anthony, and the hottest guy ever, Brock Lansing, just to name two things. Okay, so she and Brock weren't an official couple, but there was chemistry there that no one would deny. She was beyond certain that she and Miren would have a lifelong friendship, undying through the twists and turns lives navigate after being chewed up and spit out of the mouth of an award-winning, but terribly haunted, school district. *Go, fend for yourselves, young minds; you will thank us forever for preparing you for a successful life!* Or so implied the propaganda. At least their two-year stretch in Littleton had brought her and Miren together, at the right moment in time, the right space in their being.

Dipping her reflective, wire-rimmed glasses (the only ones she'd found that didn't get tangled in her long, honey-colored hair) below her eyes, revealing ice-blue orbs that always held a hint of mischief in them, she judgmentally surveyed her new home. Her Labrador pup, Coraline, followed so closely, the dog's shadow was one with her owner's. Hazel approached her twin as he walked over a sketchy wooden bridge, shaking the rickety rail, brown paint flecks falling like snow as he did.

"So, Dad—a moat? Don't see these much on HGTV," said Holden. Directing his speech to Hazel, he spoke from the side of his mouth, his perfect, white teeth, catching the sunlight as it broke free of the morning clouds. "We just need three billy goats to complete this look. I'm pretty sure there's already a hungry troll under here somewhere." He stomped his foot, reanimating the brown dust in a plume. His long hair fell onto Hazel's face as he leaned over the railing. He should have gotten that haircut back in February. If only they had known.

Hazel rolled her eyes at her brother's childish antics. "Be careful; you could be mistaken for one of those goats. You're long overdue for a shave, and you're kind of smelly," she chided as she caught sight of the length of Holden's shadow. It reached far beyond hers. Their shadowy selves were distorted by two years' worth of fallen leaves compressed into the dry creek bed below, but they couldn't hide the drastic and ever-changing disparity in their sizes. The differences between the two siblings seemed to grow as quickly as Holden did. Even biology played a part in distancing the once thick-as-thieves relationship the two had since they shared a crib. Their connection was never distant but was constantly evolving, and it had grown more evident that each of them had other people they chose more consistently to share their time with. Maybe when they took driver's education together, hopefully soon, the kinship would be revived as they shared the high school experience in a new town. There was no telling how long social distancing would remain gospel to Mom and Dad. Who knew when they'd have the opportunity to meet new people?

"Uh, yeah, it's a drainage thing, I think. There's a seasonal waterfall off the back of the property, just beyond the gazebo," Dad answered, as he struggled with the keys to the giant door.

"Come on, you guys, I'll give you the grand tour!" Mom waved impatiently, urging the teens to get a move on.

A mosquito pierced Hazel's calf with its microscopic lance. Her hand came away tacky with sweat as she eyeballed her kill lying in her palm. Spring in Oklahoma—cue the seasonal waterfall, a flying, blood-sucking bug's dream. As she strode to the front door, in no discernible rush, she realized the constant jingle of dog-tag-on-collar was not close enough to flat tire her well-worn Chucks. Coraline had not blindly followed. Her pup hadn't run off after an alien form of wildlife she had never before encountered, nor was she distracted by the onslaught of new everything assaulting her sensitive snout. Instead, the dog sat bunched with tension, crouched on the ridiculous bridge, her expressive, hazy, gilded eyes laser focused on the front door. A thick tendril of stiffened fur rose along her spine.

"Come on, girl, we don't wanna miss the grand tour." Hazel spoke to the dog in a tone that while lighthearted, carried a tinge of snark. Coraline ignored her person's call as if the command had gone unheard.

"Coraline, come," Hazel said firmly. The dog's movement was barely perceivable as she inched cautiously toward Hazel. Growing inpatient, as much with the oppressive air as with the dog, Hazel approached and gave the pup a nudge. Impatience yielded to alarm as the docile dog snapped at her with a snarl.

"Coraline, what's gotten into you? I know it's creepy, but it's home now." Taking the dog by the collar, she dragged her to the front porch.

Dad was able to get the key to work and stood at the door that had a barred hatch in place of a peephole. With a slight puffing of his chest, pride being the exhale, he announced ceremoniously, "Welcome to Weizak Manor!" He swung the door inward, ignoring the screech of metal-on-metal as the oxidized hinges struggled to function after their lengthy dormancy.

Phineas, Mom's spoiled Chihuahua, breached the threshold first, wedging himself between Mom's feet, somehow not tripping her. Mom and Dad, then Holden followed behind. Hazel didn't relax her grip on Coraline's collar as she made eye contact with the pup, silently willing her to do the walking thing on her own. The dog made no indication that entering the house voluntarily was in the cards. Lurching forward, with a tug of the collar, Hazel nearly collided with the door as it shut in her face.

The absurd hatch opened, revealing Holden's dramatically shifty green eyes. "Halt, who goes there?" he hurled the question out the over-sized opening.

"Your mom. Let me in, now!"

"Shots fired," he spoke as he closed the latch to the peephole and opened the door. "Hate to throw shade, but Weizak Manner is too extravagant for this crib. 'Ye Olde Weizak Inn' seems more appropriate. Who designed this place, Shrek? It's a bloody trip back in time, m'lady," he finished in an amazingly realistic cockney accent.

"Yeah, not so sure I get the hype." She pushed past her brother, stifling an abrupt giggle. The medieval character of the house's exterior was mimicked in the dungeon-like entryway. Sounds bounced off the stone floors and a massive staircase, echoing through Gothic, arched doorways down hallways that branched off from the preposterous foyer. The chandelier had most definitely been smuggled out of an ancient castle nestled someplace across the pond, near a foggy bog. Its heavy iron chain held a ring of faux candles. Very mid-fifteenth century chic.

Mom was already lost within the walls of the house, a flurry of excited energy. "You've got to come see this kitchen! Double ovens, Haze! Double ovens!"

Hazel set out with an air of one touring a historic landmark, not of one exploring her own home. Who in the 1980s had decided to build a house in such odd form? She followed the sounds reverberating beyond the dining room and found herself in a short hallway lined with leaded glass cabinets. Wispy gray filaments spun by spiders, hopefully long gone, seemed to appear out of nowhere, and softly tickled her face as she pressed on. "Mom, where are you? This place is whack."

As she turned corner, she was face to—well, shoulders—with Holden. "Go to the light, Carol Ann," he joked.

"Only if you aren't there," she said, skirting around him to enter the kitchen. Thankfully, this room was a bit more updated than the Dickensian kitchen she had pictured in her mind. There was no open fire with a pig on a spit, no bundles of drying herbs hanging from the beams. But it was enormous, with enough space to cook for an army, and featured an overbearing island in the middle that could seat at least six. Despite the room's size, it had a coziness that the other rooms so far had not.

"What do you think of that butler's pantry?" her mom inquired as she sidestepped Coraline, the dog rushing to the window in a huff. Beyond the picture window, which provided natural light for the dim room, the pup spotted motion and would not deny herself the opportunity to boast her protective bark.

"Quiet, Coraline," Hazel admonished, as she approached the window to see what stirred the dog's instinct. At the garden's edge, descending into the thick brush, was a flock of wild turkeys.

"Thanksgiving's going to be fresh," Holden remarked.

The view from the window left little doubt as to why Dad had been drawn to this place. A swimming pool stretched just off the expansive, stone patio. Although still covered by a thick canvas tarp, whose green hue was almost indiscernible under the thick blanket of leaves, it was easy to envision the inviting water that lay beneath. The encircling trees fed a sense of utter isolation, as if they had landed on an island, and what lay beyond was uncharted territory. The garden would need some work and the gazebo needed a fresh coat of paint. The list of projects warranted by this new acquisition seemed endless. No doubt Dad had the logistics carefully plotted on a spreadsheet somewhere on his hard drive.

"Wait till you see the laundry room!" Mom raved. "Spoiler alert ... it isn't in the kitchen!" she said with a youthful squeal. She couldn't resist taking a jab at the vastly different home they left behind in Colorado. In the two years they inhabited the solid, but small house, not a day passed that she hadn't complained about the washer and dryer being in the kitchen, as well as the tiny bathrooms and almost nonexistent closets. The pendulum swung in the opposite direction now. She could never complain about anything being too small in this house.

"Hey, guys, come check out your rooms," Dad called from upstairs, his voice sounding a million miles away, but still clear as it resounded through the barren space.

"Oh, yes, your bedrooms, and your very own bathrooms!" Mom was positively giddy. She grabbed each of the twin's hands, her eyes wide, as she dragged them back to the entryway and up the stairs.

The tour of the home took longer than any of them expected. An uneasy current of doubt settled just beyond their awareness, one that questioned whether they would ever get used to living in such a grand house. Mom and Dad's room surely identified more as a master chamber than the familiar moniker of primary suite. Holden's room, with its walls of stately, dark-wood built-ins, yearned to be filled with personal keepsakes from times gone by and leather-bound Shake-spearean tomes, but would have to be satisfied with ever-expanding collections of Funko Pop! figures, Lego Star Wars creations, and gaming merch.

Hazel's room presented her with daunting aesthetic chal-lenges. While easily twice the size of her former space, it was overwhelmed by the décor. It looked like it belonged to a toddler, one who took her first steps in the year 1547. The walls were papered in a gaudy, cream-colored, velveteen abomi-nation, except for one wall, which held an unusual mural. A talented artist had created a view of a serene meadow, ringed by a forest. With a modicum of imagination, one could easily conjure Little Red Riding Hood peeking out from behind one of the eerily realistic trees. All of it would have to go. She was almost sixteen, and this preschool nursery rhyme vibe was defi-nitely not her.

They walked through the rooms, Mom and Dad gushing all

the while about the size of the bathrooms, the master bedroom fireplace, the abundance of storage space, and so on. The tour ended in a huge room at the far end of the second floor. Had the room been inside a true Tudor mansion, it would hold antiques draped by drop cloths, chests filled with relics, and sepia photos of the lineage who once roamed the halls. This being an outlandish revival built in 1984, instead it was a vast, empty bonus room. This particular bonus room was destined to become the theater room, replete with a stand-up popcorn popper and lifted platforms for plush, mechanically reclining seats. Dad had been looking forward to having a home theater for a very long time; a place to set up his projector, huge, retractable screen and myriad of speakers. At the far end of the space, a spiral staircase provided a quick escape directly to the laundry room for anyone who couldn't be bothered walking to the main staircase.

Even the unflappable teens mustered some excitement as they discussed which movie posters would look best, Holden insisting a *Star Wars* theme was a must while Hazel argued cult classic horror movies would be best. The planning was interrupted by the doorbell, which sounded surprisingly like an average, regular doorbell, not like the foreboding church bells Hazel had imagined. She almost sighed in relief at their mediocrity.

"At last, my computer stuff!" Holden exclaimed.

"Not so fast! Give the movers space. We don't want to make them uncomfortable. And put your mask on," Mom shouted after him as he rushed down the stairs.

The twins stood outside, under a mantle of countless trees, as the moving team unloaded their lives box-by-box, piece-by-piece, from the giant truck. All of them were eager to have their creature comforts back after living for several weeks in their RV with only the barest of necessities.

As the virus began its unabated spread across Colorado, Mom and Dad decided to cut bait and head to Oklahoma as soon as the e-signatures had been accepted on the seller's documents. The plan had been to find temporary housing while finishing out the school year in Colorado after the home sold much quicker than expected. Oklahoma was still seemingly untouched by the virus, but things changed so quickly. The upheaval, one of many resulting from the pandemic, left them essentially homeless. Short-term rentals were hard to come by, and they were weeks away from closing on the Shrek house. They were forced to live in their motor home on a red dirt plot outside of Stillwater, at the height of tornado season. Thankfully, all the potentially cataclysmic events that could have taken place did not. There were constant complaints about the cramped space, the roar of the highway, and rain. Day upon day of rain that shrunk the inadequate space by feet, if not yards. Their moods were as gray as the skies as reality set in that life would not return to normal for a very long time, if ever.

The movers struggled with what appeared to be their first pandemic-ruled job, as Hazel watched and reflected on how quickly life had changed. She found it hard to believe that every single aspect of daily norms had been thrown into a tailspin, and believed she had been dealt a worse hand than many. Aside from the abrupt, unwanted move and the struggles brought about from lockdowns, she and Holden were still reeling from the changes to their academic lives. The two had been deprived of their last day of school when in-person learning was abruptly canceled in an effort to slow the spread. Mom insisted they stay home March 13th, to avoid the virus. Mom was right when she predicted that they wouldn't be returning to the halls of Heritage High School for the remainder of the year, despite the belief that the extended spring break would be enough to "flatten the curve." Hazel had pleaded with Mom and Dad to be allowed to go that day. Holden was fine with the excused absence and provided no backup for his sister's argument.

"Come on, Holden, we need to present a united front!" she had urged him.

"Uh, chill out, sis. We're talking parental mandated hooky, not war." Holden was even unfazed by the cancellation of the school play, missing the opportunity to perform on the high school stage for the first time.

Hazel hated that she had missed her last chance to hug Miren, ogle Brock in swim class, and just soak up normal life before it all came to a jarring halt. At least now they could finish out the school year in their own rooms, not in their relegated zones inside the claustrophobic walls of the motor home.

Mom did her best to direct the movers to the proper rooms without crowding them, but it did little good. In the end, most of the furniture was placed in the correct room, but the boxes would require a bit more unjumbling. Bailey, the family cat, ventured out from an unknown hiding place, as soon as the moving truck had eased its way back over the bridge and driven out of sight. The cat was cowering on the stair landing, attempting to relax enough to feast her eyes upon the multitude of tiny birds flitting about on the limbs just beyond the window. Hazel scooped up the cat and retreated to her room for some unpacking, Coraline's paws brushing her heels as she went.

TWO

By the time Hazel got her furniture arranged to her liking, and her bed put together, it was dinnertime—pizza, the official meal of moving. Mom was over the moon that her favorite college-days restaurant, The Original Hideaway, delivered all the way out to their new neighborhood of Camelot Crossing.

Hazel was starving. "Bet it takes the driver a fortnight to make it all the way out here," she told Holden.

"Fortnight? This place is already changing you, Lady Hazel." Holden responded, laughing at himself with a heartiness that vastly overreached the hilarity factor of the joke.

She was pleased to be wrong about the delivery window. The pizza arrived, piping hot, just minutes after Dad gave her a twenty and a five, asking her to put the cash on the table that sat outside the front door. "When did you become such a baller, Dad? This seems like a lot for a tip."

"Yes, but they deserve it. The stakes are higher these days for frontliners, and we are a ways out here."

The pie was some of the best any of them had ever had. And Mom was finally able to share one of her favorite items the pizza joint offered. "You haven't lived until you've had Hide-away fried mushrooms," she would say whenever she saw them on a menu. She was right. They were amazing.

Mom and Dad continued to chatter excitedly about their new home as they ate from paper plates at the kitchen island. Hazel hoped their exuberance might rub off on her as she did her best not to go down the abyss of what-ifs. Try as she might, she couldn't avoid the pointless barterer in her head who agreed that she would gladly trade this crazy mansion for their old house in Colorado. She missed her old life. This trajectory the virus had sent her on had broken the course she had vaguely developed and fully expected to fulfill: sophomore year, driver's license, Miren, Brock, spring dance, yearbook signing. She knew that as things stood, even if she was still in Colorado, everyone's old lives were a thing of the past for now. The suddenness with which the world changed was disorienting. The speed at which social beings became detainees in their own homes was appalling.

After dinner, the twins took the dogs outside for the last call of nature before bedtime. "Keep an eye on my little guy," Mom oozed in a syrupy voice. "Who knows what could be out there. Snakes, hawks, coyote!" Dramatic pause. "Stay engaged. Probably even bobcats!" And to the point, "I don't want him snatched up by a predator."

"Mom, he weighs five pounds and is barely covered by fur. He's like if male-pattern baldness hooked up with a large rat. Everything's a predator to Phin," Holden taunted. His reaction, though just for laughs, always left Mom feeling a bit more anxious about the world her beloved Phineas faced. She was never amused, certain the tiny dog looked scrumptious to anything and everything. An easy target.

Outside, the night buzzed with the electric pulse of dozens of cicadas. Their numbers would multiply by the week, overpowering all other sounds of nature. Oklahomans had no choice but to succumb to the constant hiss as spring rushed into summer. But for now, it provided soothing background noise in the absence of cars, dog walkers, sirens, and street sweepers that were a constant in Colorado and was better than the roar of the highway that shook the RV. The sky was lit by an endless veneer of fairy-light stars that seemed close enough to graze with your fingertips.

Phineas survived the nighttime outing, unharmed. Mom was right; this was the most adversarial environment Phin had ever faced. The little dog himself had been oblivious to his own peril.

Back inside, Dad made a show of checking the locks on all the doors and windows. His day had been spent installing security cameras. He was obsessed with making sure cameras caught everything once porch pirates became attuned to Mom's online shopping addiction.

They were all tired. Each one felt the fatigue differently. Dad's head ached from reading small print and hunching over protruding wires, with a voltmeter and fishing tools in hand. His burden of responsibility formed knotted tension in his neck and shoulders.

Mom's back ached, mostly due to anxiety over the workload she now faced. The house needed her undivided attention; cleaning it would take weeks, but she still had one more month of distance teaching twenty-two Pre-K kids back in Colorado. For her, living out of boxes for one minute longer than necessary was a crime. She was anxious for the challenging school year to end, so she could focus all her energy on making the house clean and comfortable. Fortunately, her own children were coasting along nicely on their own as they pioneered their way through the acute and drastic pivot. They didn't require her constant attention like many children did as they transitioned from walking hallways seven hours a day to muddling through schoolwork on a Chromebook for as many hours as they could stand. She knew from the moment the word *pandemic* became part of the daily vernacular that they wouldn't be returning to the classroom, but could have never imagined how taxing it would be to teach from afar. So while she didn't worry about helping her own kids with school, the demands of her job and setting up a new house, especially one of this size, weighed heavily on her unrested mind.

Holden was tired and sore, the sturdy teen being the newly appointed muscle of the group. (Dad abdicated the title due to bad knees and age.) But he needed some time to escape to his online world before he could sleep. In that world, nothing much had changed. Same people, same games, same banter, comfort, familiarity. No matter what they faced in the world, there was always a wormhole, and he would always be accepted by the group. There was no concern with fitting in; all their pieces fit together just fine, and had since kindergarten. Despite his fatigue, Holden eagerly set about building his wired world so he could rejoin his friends.

Hazel's heart ached more than her body. When the movers brought the last of their belongings into the house, finality washed over her like a crushing wave. She was over 600 miles away from her comfort zone. Did anyone in her family even comprehend how difficult it was for a fifteen-year-old girl to find a comfort zone in the first place?

There would be no first kiss from Brock Lansing. That crushed dream was one of many. But she and Miren texted and FaceTimed relentlessly, so while there were no more weekends spent secondhand scavenger shopping at the Arc Thrift Store, no long lunches spent people watching from the window seat at Pho Real, and no free blocks spent studying on the lawn at Heritage High School, they were still connected.

The family ascended the stairs together to prepare for their first night in the Shrek house. Due to their exhaustion, bedtime came much earlier than most recent nights since morning commutes were no longer a thing. As they reached the second-floor landing, Dad said, "Well, here we go, family. Finally sleeping in rooms of our own!"

"I don't know how I will sleep without the peaceful melody of your snoring, Haze," Holden jabbed.

"Yeah, I'll certainly miss being woken up every morning at three when you make your nightly bathroom trip, loser," Hazel retorted.

"Get some rest. Tomorrow is going to be another busy day," Mom said, rooting for them all. "I put fresh towels in your bathrooms. Feel free to come get me or drop in if you need anything."

Dad nudged Mom into their bedroom, saying, "They aren't babies anymore. They don't need to be tucked in with one more story and a glass of water." Over his shoulder, he whispered, "Sweet dreams," as he turned off the hall light and closed the door behind him.

THREE

It wasn't even 9:30 when Hazel climbed into bed. It felt much later. She checked her Snap, and texted Miren to see if she could FaceTime. Her eyelids grew heavier as she relaxed, waiting for a reply. It had only been a few minutes, but the comfort of finally climbing into her own bed soothed her, and she knew it was time to call it. She sent another text.

L: **Can't keep eyes open. Must sleep. Tmr we FaceTime. Can't wait to show u the castle. U won't believe this place.**

As the pillow cushioned her head, and she wiggled her body into a comfortable position, a faint beeping sound disrupted the quiet. It was followed by the unmistakable sound of footfalls running down the long hallway. Coraline's response to the ruckus was immediate and fierce. The dog bolted from her sleep, fur lifting along her spine. A deep growl grew in the dog's throat.

Hazel's ears tracked the sound as the runner reached the end of the hall and rushed headlong down the staircase. Then it stopped. Silence returned and tension fell away from the dog as she dropped her guarded stance and rolled to her back with a whimper.

"Coraline, stay," Hazel whispered, throwing the blankets back and getting out of bed. She didn't know what she'd find outside as she pulled her hoodie tightly around herself in a subconscious effort to smooth the goosebumps that popped up on her arms and legs. Hopefully Mom and Dad were already on the job, admonishing their errant son, condemning his childish behavior.

The vast blackness of the unfamiliar hallway gave her pause. Every door was closed, hiding whatever might be lurking beyond its threshold. As she considered ignoring the whole thing, granting her brother a reprieve by going back to bed, the friendly, staccato voice of Alexa echoed through the house.

"Motion detected at the garage door."

She flinched, and the disruption to the heavy silence caused curiosity to dissolve into fear. They couldn't actually be experiencing a break-in on their first night, could they? Unable to move and unsure of what to do, she froze, awaiting the arrival of Mom and Dad, certain they would respond to the warning from the Ring. She remained alone in the cavernous hallway. None of it made sense. Who had run down the hall? Who was outside the garage door, and could they be inside by now? And why was no one else coming to investigate?

An eerie blue glow emanated from the space under Holden's door. While it looked ominous in a very mad-scientist-at-work kind of way, she knew it was from the multiple monitors he used for Discord and gaming. She crept closer to his door, her wide-eyed gaze bouncing from surface to surface, knowing anything she saw might require her immediate reaction. Standing outside his room, she could now hear his laughter and chatter. She knocked on his door.

"Enter if you must," he responded instinctively more than cognitively.

She was met with a disarray of partially unpacked boxes, but his elaborate gaming system was completely set up on the built-in desktop. He hadn't even put his bedding on his bed. Priorities.

Holden didn't break from his game when she entered, his fingers feverishly tapping as his hands toggled back and forth on the keyboard and mouse in a blur. He slid one headphone off his ear and asked, "What?"—not hiding his annoyance with the interruption. Obviously, he wouldn't have noticed the earlier commotion with his ears fully engulfed in the oversized headset.

"Never mind," she said, leaving the room.

No way she was going to fall asleep until she got some answers. She inched farther down the hall, past Holden's room to her parents' door. How could they be oblivious to these events? They were supposed to be responsible adults. Going downstairs to investigate a potential intruder lurking about was a task no teenage girl should face alone under the best of circumstances. Doing so in this huge, creepy, unfamiliar house was out of the question. From beyond the bedroom door, a twenty-four-hour news network's talking head rattled off the day's grim stories. She knocked.

Mom came to the door, "Hey, Haze, what's up?"

Phineas tunneled his way out from under the covers where he had been sleeping at the foot of the bed and gave a half-hearted bark, warning Mom of a potential intruder at her door approximately sixty seconds too late. A keen sense of hearing and protective instincts had never quite been developed in the canine. He had also been oblivious to the person running outside the door mere minutes ago.

"Did you hear all that?" Hazel asked, waving her arm

behind her to indicate where the noises had come from but keeping her eyes on Mom.

Mom stood on her toes, peering over Hazel's shoulder as if she could *see* the sounds Hazel was talking about. "Hear what?"

Hazel's eyes blinked rapidly, and she shook her head in disbelief, as if her family's lack of awareness was being tossed in her face.

Dad leaned out of the bathroom, his electric toothbrush still churning in his mouth, and attempted to say, "What's going on?"

"Hazel's having some first-night jitters, that's all," Mom said to Dad. Turning back to Hazel, and using her practiced there-there-dear voice, she said, "I was using my WaterPik. I didn't hear anything. This house has been vacant a long time. I'm sure it has some settling to do."

"But the Ring ... Motion ... Garage door ..."

"Yeah, Dad checked the app. He couldn't see anything, really. He said there was a flash of light and then maybe some fog. It shouldn't have triggered the sensor. It may be some malfunction, I don't know. He said he would check it out tomorrow. Maybe it was an animal, but it's certainly no masked home invader. There's nothing to worry about." Mom was rambling in an obvious effort to calm her daughter's nerves.

Seeing her family's reaction, or lack thereof, Hazel almost believed the settling house theory. "Um, yeah, okay. Sorry to bother you guys. Good night."

"No bother. You know, you should try Sleep Sounds on your Dot. It's the best. It blocks out noises, like snoring," she said in a low, conspiratorial whisper. Winking, she nodded her head toward the bathroom where Dad could be heard gargling mouthwash. "Always helps me nod off."

Dad exited the bathroom and joined the conversation. "I'll

take a look at the Ring camera out back tomorrow. Probably needs some adjusting. Sleep tight, kid," he said.

Hazel hugged her mom and left the room. Back in the hallway, she stomped her foot to mimic the noise only she and her dog had heard just minutes ago. With a shrug, she returned to her room, bracing herself for a jump scare to emerge from the shadows. But nothing was lurking in the recesses.

A sleeping Coraline roused and lifted her head without alarm. The dog had moved past it. Hazel tapped the tops of boxes, scanning for one labeled *L's Nightstand*. The small, round device was on the top, inside hastily wadded, gray paper. She plugged it in, waited for the ringed light to flash, then directed, "Alexa, play Sleep Sounds." The intensity of the day swept her away swiftly. In an instant she was under sleep's spell.

FOUR

The speed at which a life can be reborn in a new setting is astounding. The next day, the family shaped the space together full tilt, melding old memories with new lives, each doing their part to nestle into their forever home. It was enormous task that found them working late into the evening.

Leftover pizza, the official dinner of moving day number two.

Dad tossed a partially eaten wedge of crust back onto his paper plate. Slowly circling his neck and shoulders, he said, "I'm back on the clock tomorrow. I need some additional muscle; my office furniture is too much for this old man to handle by himself. Any volunteers willing to help a dad out? I'll pay you in pizza."

His request was met with reluctant, but obligatory groans of acceptance from Hazel and Holden. "You both look pretty able-bodied to me," Mom said, gathering the remnants of their meal.

Thankfully Dad's office was on the ground floor, and they

reconvened in decidedly the most baffling room in the house. It had a stained-glass window with a family-crest vibe, and a Romeo and Juliet balcony from whence Mom could summon her minions, should she so desire. The mash-up of elements resulted in the room bearing resemblance to a Vegas-style chapel where the black sheep of Tudor families could have a quickie wedding. They decided to call it the cathedral. "Dad's office" was far too bland for such a grandiose design.

Dad and Holden heaved the heavy oak desk across the sea of parquet, being careful not to scratch it, under Mom's vigilant eye. Hazel focused on the landmass jutting out halfway up the immense wall. "Why is there a balcony with no stairs?" she pondered out loud. The only reply was the sound of successive footfalls overhead. In unison, their wide-eyed gazes shifted to the ceiling. Sharp intakes of air could be heard, and they all held their breaths as the noise boomed on.

Both dogs heard the noise and reacted by cowering, whimpering high-pitched sounds from behind bared teeth. The maelstrom died down as the unseen runner reached the bottom of the stairs. The dulling thud of feet treading on the stone entry floors could be heard briefly. Finally, the silence broke the trance that held them all. Together they advanced into the foyer, stepping over both dogs, who were now positioned as if anticipating belly rubs and whining in harmony.

"That! That was it! The noise I heard last night!" Hazel urged.

Dad grabbed the banister at the foot of the stairs and stared up the dark staircase. "What was that?"

Mom peered over his shoulder, clutching his T-shirt. She started to say something, but was interrupted by Alexa announcing, "Motion detected at the garage door."

They followed Dad into the kitchen to see what the

watchful eye outside the garage door saw. The Echo Show screen was lit up, a grainy flurry of moths dancing chaotically, their virtual auras lit by an unnatural glow of night vision. "I made adjustments again today. I guess they weren't enough," he mumbled in puzzlement as he visualized his actions, replaying each step, checking them off in the eye of his mind.

"Squirrels?" Mom questioned, wide-eyed and hopeful.

"Um, sure, if they make squirrels the size of large children out here in the sticks," Holden jabbed.

Mom's frigidly stern expression, fondly referred to by all as "the look," flashed in Holden's direction. Dad enveloped Mom in his arms, saying, "I'll call a critter company tomorrow and have it checked out. It wouldn't be too unusual to have some unwanted guests in the attic. They've had free rein of the place for a long time."

Mom was pacified by this action plan, and the two returned to the cathedral arm-in-arm to finish arranging Dad's office. Holden waited a beat to see if he would be summoned again. When he heard soft giggles and banter from the room behind him, he shrugged at Hazel. "I think our work here is done," he said, making his escape up the stairs. As he reached the top stair, he turned and stomped down again, bringing to life the unmistakable sound of feet pounding down the stairs. Holden, though swallowed up by the darkness, yelled, "Gotcha!"

Hazel was glad he didn't see her flinch, or know that given another half a second, she would have turned and run back to the cathedral to the comfort of other people. "Not funny, lame-o!" she said, attempting to smooth out any unease her voice might betray. "Heading up to bed," she called to Mom and Dad.

"Good night, sweetie!" Mom piped back.

Just like that, all returned to normal and complacency thwarted the hunt for a rational explanation. No one had noted the time when they'd heard the noises, but from the moment the pounding started to the time they went their separate ways, fewer than ten minutes had passed. The entire exchange became a moment in the past by 10:07 p.m.

FIVE

Dad hired a man whose truck boasted the clever moniker, *Critter Getters*. Dave Rogers, said getter of critters, arrived two days later to assess the infestation of giant squirrels. The family left out the part about the rodents being a genius bunch who were able to throw their scurrying sounds, making it sound as if they were running helter-skelter on the second floor before plummeting down the stairs. There was never any indication of the clandestine gang having fled the scene via the garage door, but the unblinking eye of the Ring camera continued its nightly alert despite Dad's daily efforts to manipulate the settings. A flash of light and a hazy fog were always detected upon playback.

"Oh, yeah. An empty house can be taken over in the space of weeks. A shrewd gaze can establish a bona fide flop house for wildlife in two years' time. Fun fact, a group of raccoon is called a gaze," the lanky man informed the family after learning of the extended absence of human life inside the house. "But I'll fix you up. Rest assured when I'm done, every entry point will be sealed up and any stowaways will be cast out. Eventually they'd take off on their own, anyway. They aren't too keen on the smells we humans and our four-legged friends produce," he noted, scratching Coraline behind her ear. "I can expedite their eviction though. They can be stubborn."

From the family room, Hazel overheard the conversation that took place just beyond the huge French doors, on the fresh-aired safety of the back porch. Never had she given thought to the dynamics of raccoon and their wiles. Dave tipped his hat at her as he entered the house and passed by, donning his mask and setting about to rid the house of its noisy intruders. Mom followed him, maintaining six feet of distance, her mouth and nose hidden behind a mask as well.

"Dave," she said in a muffled voice, "I found a scorpion in the kitchen the other day!" News to Hazel. "What would I do if one of us stepped on one, or my Phineas got stung?" She trailed after the man, leaving Hazel alone again in the living room. Hazel scanned the floor in front of her, slipped off her slides and tucked her feet safely beneath her hips. She could hear Dave placate Mom as she followed him upstairs to begin his search, and couldn't contain an eye roll. A loud screech could be heard upstairs and Hazel was certain Dave had escaped Mom's inquiries. There was no way Mom would venture into a musty, infested attic space.

Fluffy, pink tufts of fiberglass insulation clung to Dave's close-cropped, blond hair, and he wiped away a layer of sweat, taking with it two shades of his skin tone. "Well, there's nothing inside the walls. The attic is clear. Maybe they're content outside and use your roof as passage from point A to point B. They're creatures of habit; you could set a clock to their schedules."

If Dave had hung around, waited for the sun to set, and had a chance to hear what happened on the stairs every night at 10 o'clock, he would have eaten his words. But they were not experts and reluctantly accepted his explanation. Of course, they hadn't mentioned that a beeping stopwatch announced the nightly run. Nor had they asked how vermin could trigger the motion detector outside the garage, from the roof, while remaining undetected. But he did say they were shrewd. Shrewd and undeterred, the nightly occurrence continued, never veering from its predictable course.

Maybe their minds were too overburdened by the radical disunion of collective daily lives. The upended world was rife with unprecedented turns of events subliminally skewing their rationale, allowing them to easily accept another doubt-inspiring change. Soon, many mysterious things would relinquish the stair run to little more than a benign occurrence. Their first week in the Shrek house would prove uneventful in the face of what was to come. The worldly surprises they woke to each day were overshadowed by more ominous events ramping up within the presumed safety of their home.

SIX

Taking the animals to the vet provided Mom and Hazel a chance to venture out, if only to watch the world from the car window and wonder how much change had been brought upon the person in the next car over at a stop light, or the student bicycling down the sidewalk. Hazel would take it, even if sitting in Mom's car outside Dr. Strom's office was as much of the outside world as she was allotted.

Dr. Strom was a one-woman show. Her practice was previously based on the appealing lure and convenience of providing house calls. Now the parking lot was her waiting room, with limited contact preventing exposure to the virus. Each patient's caregiver was more anxious than the patient as they handed their beloved pet over to the dogged professional. It was telling that pets seemed less stressed waiting in the car than they ever had in the days of cajoling them into a waiting room sodden with scents both chemical and organic. Maybe vet waiting rooms could be avoided when the world returned to normal.

Coraline was the first to be led away. The pup, too inexperienced to resist, willingly and gleefully allowed Dr. Strom to take her leash and followed amiably. Her trust was no doubt betrayed behind the exam room door as she was poked and prodded. She exited with a clean bill of health and with concoctions already coursing through her veins, beginning to strengthen her immune system, making it more resilient.

"She did great!" the doctor said as the dog scurried to the sanctuary of the car.

Phineas, more jaded and suspicious than his younger cohort, resisted to the extent that his tiny body could. He burned untold calories as the vet carried his quivering body away from the protective arms of Mom. The dog vanished behind the door. Hazel and Mom remained in the car.

"I should have done this before this pandemic," Mom muttered, berating herself while nervously tapping the steering wheel. "I just got so busy with work. If I had known ..." She trailed off, shaking her head.

"He was eager to get out of there," said the vet, returning Phineas through the open car window. His tremors would not subside till long after the harrowing solo visit. His teeth needed cleaning, so an appointment was set. Mom handed over Bailey, the last to be examined. The cat let out a yowl of disapproval as the crate passed hands. The doctor paused briefly, providing Mom with a pamphlet of first aid tips for canine scorpion stings.

Dr. Strom's cheerful mask could not hide her somber expression as she returned with Bailey. "Can we speak privately?" she asked as she handed the crate over. Mom got out of the car. Hazel cooed to the cat in soothing tones before focusing her attention on the impromptu conference taking place beyond the car's hood. Conversations were harder to decipher these days, even if you were one of the participants. It was impossible to glean any bits of the discussion, but there was no doubt the news was not good.

Mom handed over her credit card and climbed back in the car. She immediately pumped out an overabundance of sanitizer, rubbing her hands together vigorously, slathering the caustic-smelling gel almost up to her elbows. She removed her mask and turned to Hazel. "Dr. Strom says Bailey doesn't have much longer," she said, her voice shaking. "Cancer, she thinks. At her age, there isn't much that can be done. She's putting her on some special food. It costs an arm and a leg; your Dad is going to flip." She opened a small, brown paper bag and removed blue prescription bottles one-by-one. "A steroid, antibiotics, pain pills," she rattled off. "The plan is to keep her comfortable. She is almost seventeen years old. She's led a pretty good life for a street rescue." A tear slipped down her face, absorbed quickly by the mask that now bearded her chin.

Hazel was in tears before her mom finished speaking. Bailey had been a constant in her life since before her young mind had developed memories. Mom and Dad had adopted the cat before she and Holden were born. How many times had she noted the changes in the cat's appearance and mood, and the weight loss? She had flippantly written off her concerns as stress, and had been certain Bailey would rebound once they were settled. What would life be like without Bailey's incessant meows when she wasn't fed on time? Without her loud purrs as she kneaded her way into Hazel's lap, despite all obstacles? Hazel made a silent vow to shower Bailey with extra attention and love in her remaining days.

Melancholy shrouded them all. Holden and Dad took the news about Bailey's decline badly, as expected. Bailey's imminent passing was another blow dealt by the cruel hand of 2020. Mom wasn't up to cooking that evening, so dinner was ordered in.

Dad scanned the usual spots where cash was left lying around haphazardly, and left two ten-dollar bills outside.

Through the safety of an app, he instructed the driver to leave their meal, take the tip, and ring the bell. There was little conversation as they ate. Everyone but Hazel retreated upstairs after tossing the paper bags and plastic utensils.

Hazel stayed back to tend to Bailey. The cat happily accepted the prolonged petting session and inhaled the extra portion of the pricey new food. Finally tiring of the day and the coddling, Bailey gracefully leaped to the top of the dryer and curled herself into a tiny ball. She was asleep in moments. The cat never allowed herself to be closed in a room at night, no matter how comfortable the bed and how pleasant the company might be. If she found herself sequestered behind closed doors, she would caterwaul tirelessly until she succeeded in waking the occupant, demanding to be released. Bailey preferred to roam the house at night, a prowling sentinel.

Over the next weeks, Hazel kept her promise and doted on the cat, probably more than the cat liked. She ordered a fluffy blanket covered in mice and paw prints from Mom's Amazon Prime account. The cat seemed appreciative of the cushion atop her perch on the dryer. The food and the medications seemed to help. Within days her fur regained its sheen. She looked fluffier, felt heavier. But even though she never showed any signs of discomfort, the light was leaving her eyes. There were no reserves of energy that allowed her to prowl the house in the dark. Never again did she pick a playful skirmish with Phineas. She had to be coaxed down from the dryer to eat. Even with these outward signs, Hazel couldn't admit that the pampering and medical regimen would soon cease to be enough to combat the stubborn opponent of age and disease.

SEVEN

As the seasons transitioned, steamy spring gave way to steamier summer, and the Shrek house began to look as if it had been lived in for some time. Everything found a place. Smiling photos hung from the walls, knickknacks rested in just the right spots, and furniture was situated comfortably. The space was sparse, since the furniture they owned was not enough to fill the grand house. Perhaps when the elusive curve was flattened and the pandemic was a thing of the past, they could spend their days browsing furniture stores and pick out things to make the house more homey, but for now they would make do. They each gravitated to different obligations to pass the time, which seemed warped and surreal as the world struggled to live with the unseen enemy.

Dad worked on readying the pool, urged on by the imaginings of its grand opening. The family eagerly awaited the moment he announced it was ready to cool, entertain, and exercise their bodies. Although he considered himself capable of tending to the balance of chemicals and had an innate awareness of water levels, this pool presented issues he had never faced. It had been some time since his senses were honed to the slightest turn of an additive. The curtain of tangled woods provided a vastly different backdrop than the scant shade of three palm trees they splashed about under while in their Arizona pool. The dense foliage made maintenance much more difficult, but it was a welcome distraction from working at home and kept him from devoting too much time to his job.

His family underestimated his efforts. Ignorantly blissful, they rendered their bodies to the crystal waters. Dad made sure there was no hint of the rescued frog, no fallen leaves, and chased off tiny salamanders so the image was inviting and pristine. He did regale them with creepy stories when something extraordinary popped up. He'd become concerned by the increasing prevalence of furry tarantulas and mother wolf spiders who harbored hundreds of eight-legged offspring on their backs as they transgressed its cement shores. Mom excused herself and left them room when he spoke of the scorpions and their nightly exodus from the forest. He questioned their instincts because once at the water's edge they plummeted its depths, never again reaching the surface.

Mom honed a newfound skill: procuring supplies in the wake of the pandemic, an effort which proved exacting at times since the supply chain was oddly impacted by the virus. While she longed for weekends spent shopping and lunching, she couldn't understand why anyone would go inside stores and restaurants when everything could be delivered to your car or your front door. She graciously accepted substitutes and shrugged off unavailable items in a display of sacrifice, doing what she could for the greater good. In an uncanny flash of foresight, she had stockpiled enough toilet paper, the golden goose of the modern plague, long before the hoard purchasing began. All the while, she was aware that these difficulties were a minor nuisance given the bigger picture.

Her teaching, if it could even be called that, had become a chore. There was little delight in the attempt to keep notoriously short attention spans engaged. Parents were overwhelmed, trying to work at home, or worse holding down a job outside the home, all while trying to educate their own children. It was unsustainable. The morning check-ins that started with the off-key, out of sync singing of "Hello Friends" was about as much as her young students could muster. They rarely stuck around for virtual Circle Time.

With less time spent on lesson plans and shopping trips, Mom became transfixed by the news and sat in front of the TV, unblinking, absorbed by the onslaught of devastating reports. Over dinner, she spouted statistics of death counts, hospitalizations, and infection rates. Often, meals ended in tears as she found herself sharing the stories of the lost souls.

"You need to step away from the television and social media," Dad implored. "Find some healthier distractions. We are lucky to be able to work from home. We're doing everything right, staying safe. Be grateful, and unplug. It will do you good."

Shaking her head, she would counter, "We need to stay informed. Every other day new guidelines are dispensed. There's so much chaos and death. I don't know what this world is coming to."

The twins focused on finishing up the most insane school year of their lives. They struggled to decipher assignments. The distortion of learning from a screen while sitting in a place that was far too comfortable required extra energy to not lose focus. Their faces flushed for classmates who were busted for surrendering to distractions or fell victim to an unmuted mic.

Hazel and Holden learned that their district would dispense a simple Pass or Fail in each class, which would deprive them of hard-earned As or under-the-wire Bs. Both had worked hard, and this decision would discredit their efforts. It was painfully apparent that their teachers were grappling with distance learning even more than the students. Buzzwords like pivot and grace were thrown around with abandon.

The walls were closing in on Hazel. She wanted to get out and explore her new town, even if it was one in which she did not want to be, nor felt she belonged. Her longing to be back in Colorado with her friends hit like a gut punch sometimes, knocking the air right out of her. Deflated by it all, she often cried herself to sleep. The race to end distance learning and tending to Bailey kept the homesickness at bay during waking hours. But at night, usually after catching up with Miren, the isolation and loneliness crushed her. She envied her brother's acceptance of their current situation. He was never lonely in his online world and was oblivious to her pain. She missed the cadence of the life she lived not long ago, the energy of doing things and seeing people.

There were too many hours left after a day of online school and favorite pastimes like TikTok, Twitch, and Animal Crossing became less appealing. Hazel picked up her paint-brushes and made attempts to rediscover her love of creating, but often felt uninspired and stuck. Even mundane chores made her feel somewhat useful, but time seemed to pass differently in quarantine. Every day was the same; they all just blended together, creating confusion and doubt.

Did I take out the trash yesterday? Or was it today?

The last day of school, traditionally a momentous event and the cause for dinner out at a favorite restaurant, simply passed quietly, barely recognized by a collective sigh of relief. Surprise, the twins passed! No one would ever know how impressive their passing grades actually were. Never had they imagined a world without finals, the spring dance, senior prank week, or yearbooks. Mom didn't have the chance to watch her Pre-K class graduate. It wasn't fair.

Hazel and Mom chose the pool as their favorite time-killer. Amazon rushed water workout gear to Mom. She looked ridiculous in her goggles, webbed gloves, and flotation belt. But she busied her mind and her body with a routine.

"Vitamin D provides protection from the virus," she espoused. Locked inside their small world, the virus would have to knock on their door for them to catch it. The amount of vitamin D in their systems would have little impact due to their isolation.

As Hazel floated around the pool, flipping over every fifteen minutes to maintain an even tan, her mind tortured her with thoughts of how different life should be. Sunbathing at the pool with Miren would be endlessly more entertaining than listening to Mom's '80s tunes and audible rep count.

Hazel and Mom had developed a deep, bronze skin tone by the day Mom's Amazon Music account went rogue. Mom suited up for her aquatic workout in the shade of the gazebo.

"Alexa, play my '80s playlist," she shouted at her phone as she made her way to the water. The Bluetooth speaker came to life with a song by Tears for Fears, "Mad World." After completing her routine, she emerged from the water, removed the belt and gloves, then returned to the pool, taking float on an air-filled mat. Something nagged at her during her workout, but it wasn't until her focus shifted from her routine to relaxation that the vexing source of her discomfort became apparent. She realized she was humming along to "Mad World" again. As the song wound down into its dreamy outro, she anticipated the panning warble from the intro of "Memories Fade," another Tears for Fears song. She predicted the next song correctly. Both songs were great, but they weren't the only two songs on her voluminous '80s playlist.

She paddled to the side of the pool, climbed the ladder, and went to her phone. At the same time, Hazel came out the back door, towel in hand. Mom waved her over. "Come here and tell me I'm not losing my mind!"

Hazel sensed a setup, and wished she could back up and change plans. Instead, she went to her Mom, registering the final sax solo and haunting drum beat of an old song, a favorite of Mom's. The next song in the queue was "Mad World." Mom wasn't a child of the '80s, but it was her favorite decade of music and Hazel had been subjected to the retro tunes all her life.

Mom held a finger to her lips as Hazel stood in confused silence, listening to the song, which she had to admit she kind of liked. The lilting notes of the next song began. Mom looked at her wide-eyed. Hazel was beginning to believe she would have to inform Mom that she might, in fact, be losing her mind. She wasn't ready to have Mom committed, so she started, "Tears for—"

"Ssshhh!" Mom swatted at her.

The two stood, waiting for "Memories Fade" to end, and when it did it was followed by "Mad World" again. Now Hazel got it, and she understood what had Mom so worked up. Alexa, or more correctly Amazon Music, was stuck in a loop, repeating the two songs continually. Hazel took her Mom's phone and checked her playlist, convinced Mom had made a boomer-esque error and created a playlist consisting of only two songs.

"Weird, right?" Mom said in a tone that suggested this was not user error.

"Yeah, sorta," Hazel replied, hitting the back button several times. The app's history showed the two songs repeating as far back as she cared to view. She handed the phone back over and said, "Probably just some glitch. Shut it down and reboot."

"We can just listen to one of your playlists."

"Mom, you've said my music makes you cry for today's youth. I'm not sure—"

"Well, it's better than listening to the same two songs over and over again," she said, cutting Hazel off.

"Valid point."

Mom shut her phone down and Hazel connected to the Bluetooth device. For the first time ever, Mom listened to Hazel's playlist without complaint as the two relaxed in the pool.

EIGHT

With summer officially in full swing, Hazel turned her attention to her bedroom makeover. Mom and Dad told her she was in charge, giving her the freedom to make decisions and changes as she saw fit. Their only caveat was that she had to do the majority of the work on her own. Dad would bankroll the project, Mom was project coordinator and assistant, but Hazel was the designer and most importantly, laborer. She was down with those terms.

In an attempt to downplay the romper room vibe, she had covered the walls in tapestries and art. As the wall hangings came down, she took her first good look at the mural. The room must have been intended to be a nursery, but how could it have been one for so many years? Any kids who lived here had to have outgrown the storybook image come to life on their bedroom wall. While she was put off by the juvenile feel of the mural, she was impressed by the artistry. The detail was incredible. Having dabbled in painting herself, she understood how much time and effort had been dedicated to creating the piece.

The intricacies of each blade of grass and delicacies of

every tiny flower petal were stunning. A fawn on the edge of a brook was lifelike, and the brook itself appeared to be in motion. She counted the dragonflies and ladybugs and marveled that each insect was different in color and shade, spots and details. As she admired the wall, she started feeling guilty about painting over something that someone had obviously poured their heart into. She thought about how she would feel if some kid came along and painted over something she had spent weeks creating. She didn't have the heart to obliterate the piece. Maybe others who had found respite in this room felt the same, too overcome by guilt at the thought of erasing the unknown person's craft.

Hazel decided there were ways she could camouflage it while she called the room hers. Mom and Dad planned on living there forever, but she did not. The frumpy wallpaper would definitely go and if the mural bothered her too much, she could simply cover it up again with tapestries. She would learn to live with it and use the mural as inspiration for her bedroom makeover color palette.

As she flopped onto the bed and opened her MacBook to search paint colors, her mind drifted. The project would be a much-needed distraction as she struggled with this "new normal." She knew she had it much better than so many other people, but she still couldn't come to terms with the radical changes, the things the world had taken for granted. Things "taken for granted" might be the understatement of the year. She missed Miren and couldn't quite remember Brock's face anymore. Closing her eyes to recall his dimples, she wondered how he was handling isolation.

She wanted to go to downtown Stillwater, check out the university's Student Union, meet kids her age while soaking in what life in the small town would be like. She knew she wasn't the only one who wanted these things. And so she accepted the rules for living through the pandemic for what they were and dreamed, like many, of the days when it was over, and she could hug Miren again, sit in the sun-drenched annex of the Student Union with new friends and maybe set her sights on a new guy.

She went down the online shopping rabbit hole, urges to click on the next link taking her to yet another Boho macramé wall hanging too overwhelming to deny. How would she ever decide on just one? She dozed off early and forgot to check on Bailey. She even slept through the nightly stompfest outside her room and although Coraline did not, she slept through Coraline's reaction to it.

NINE

Waking in a dazed confusion that stemmed from falling asleep unexpectedly, without following her typical bedtime routine, Hazel groggily attempted to gain her bearings. It was much earlier than she was used to. Coraline snored lightly by her side and the house was tranquil. She bolted upright as she realized that she hadn't given Bailey extra attention and food the night before. Coraline didn't stir as she exited her room. It was too early for the dog to bother getting up for her morning call of nature trip outside and bowl of kibble, so she stayed in bed, barely acknowledging Hazel's rushed departure.

Hazel sensed something different the second she entered the laundry room. The air felt and smelled differently. Bailey would usually stretch, arch and mew when the lights were turned on, but this morning Hazel was greeted with silence and stillness. The cheery blanket was atop the dryer, but there was no motion. Bracing herself, she slowly approached, calling Bailey's name in the singsong high-pitched voice all pet owners use in times of coaxing. Still, there was no motion, no meow.

As she got closer, her heart pounded as she saw the fuzzy

blanket was hiding a motionless mound. The throw was lovingly tucked around the cat, as if someone wanted to hide it. Hazel knew that something had to be wrong; Bailey would never lay there covered so tightly. She wasn't one of those cats who liked to be under the covers—she had to be outside the blankets, always aware of her surroundings, not wanting to be vulnerable. They chalked it up to her life before being rescued. Hazel had to tug on the blanket as it was tucked so intently and securely, weighted down by an unmoving mass. There, under the blanket, was Bailey's lifeless body. At first the cat appeared to be sleeping, but she was taking no breaths. She was gone.

Tears sprung forth and a tiny, gasping cry escaped Hazel's lips. Poor Bailey! Hazel had failed to tend to the cat last night. Too wrapped up in her stupid musings, she had ignored her frail, dying cat. How could she be such a careless person? She had left Bailey to die alone! How could she ever forgive herself? Pain ripped through her, shocking her system with overwhelming grief. Her heart ached and the tears leaked through her clenched eyes while she made no sound other than gasping inhales.

Hazel could not bring herself to touch the cat now in her state of death. She was afraid. Afraid of what her beloved cat would feel like. She didn't know what to do, so she sunk to the floor, crying harder.

She wasn't sure how long she had been there crouched on the cold, hard floor sobbing below her dead cat before Mom came in. Mom was humming a tune. In the back of her mind, Hazel recognized the song, "Mad World." Mom reached into a cabinet and pulled out a box of K-cups, oblivious to her daughter's presence.

"Oh, you scared me!" She jumped, covering her mouth and dropping the box. Her shock was tossed aside when she saw the tears running down Hazel's red face. "Sweetie, what's wrong?"

Hazel said nothing but Mom's gaze landed above her daughter's head, to the mound on top of the dryer. "Is she? No!" Mom choked on her words as she struggled to fathom what she was seeing.

Hazel dropped her head as Mom sat beside her, wrapping her arms around her daughter. She gently pulled Hazel's head to her shoulder and the two sat in their sadness. The day that had been promised had come, and Bailey was gone. Mom was crushed by the loss of her long-time companion; her emptiness belied her maternal instinct to comfort her child.

Hazel nestled her face in Mom's hair and fought to speak without the halting gasps that made her feel like a child, but she lost that battle. "Why did you guys just cover her up and leave her here?" she managed to say.

"What do you mean?" Mom asked in confusion.

Hazel stood, wanting to show her mom how the cat had laid in repose, but couldn't bring herself to do it, as it meant touching her departed cat, acknowledging the evidence. She turned her back and said, "When I found her, she was completely covered by her blanket. She couldn't have wrapped herself up that way; it was tucked all the way around her."

"Oh no, Haze, I would have never left her here for you to come upon." Mom contemplated the scene briefly, wiped her face and exited the room to set about understanding how the cat became enshrouded and forgotten.

Hazel didn't know what to do with herself, but she couldn't leave the cat alone. She checked the garage door. It was locked, of course. She felt foolish even as she was doing it. Like someone would come in and give the cat her last rites in the middle of the night! Dad had been hypervigilant about doors, especially this door as it was the closest one to the source of the puzzling nightly camera alert.

Mom returned with Dad by her side, looking visibly shaken

and reluctant to accept the reality. Ever the stoic one, Dad tried to hide the tears welling up, threatening to spill over. "Poor, Bailey. Why don't you two leave me to this? I'll find a box we can use for a coffin."

Hazel was grateful for the pass to escape the room, knowing Bailey wouldn't be alone. As she turned to go, she asked, "Can you leave her wrapped in her blanket?" She knew it was a silly request but wanted Bailey to be comfortable in her resting spot.

Dad nodded, "Sure thing, Haze."

Torment seized her chest again, escaping in a feeble whimper as Mom ushered her out of the room. They could hear Dad whispering loving words of goodbye to their family member.

Dad emerged to find his wife and daughter sitting at the kitchen island. He felt the brunt of their pain more strongly than the sadness of his own loss. "I found the perfect box," he said, realizing those words provided no comfort. "I'm going to check in with Holden, see if he knows anything."

Hazel followed, needing to find out if Holden had left the cat without a mention. She knew it was unlikely; he wasn't heartless. She sat on the landing bench and watched as Dad knocked on Holden's door, waking him. Dad entered and from behind the door she could hear the murmurs of conversation, deciphering only one syllable from Holden.

"No!" he said, as Dad delivered the grim account.

As Dad exited Holden's room, Hazel caught a glimpse of her brother, head in hands, and heard the disturbed intake of breath as he lost the ability to stifle his tears.

Dad sat next to Hazel and followed her gaze out the window. "Holden never went back downstairs after dinner last night," he said.

Slowly, dreamily, she replied, "Yeah, I knew he wouldn't have done that. But who did?"

"I saw her on top of the dryer when I checked the locks last night. She seemed fine. I petted her for a few minutes, and she mustered a purr," he recounted.

Father and daughter sat in silence for some time, their hearts becoming heavier as the acceptance set in. Dad spoke first, breaking the dull silence. "I need to get back to work. When you are up to it, you and your brother should find a nice spot to bury her. We'll have a little service later today. She deserves something nice, I think."

Hazel nodded as Dad went through the ghastly list of suggestions of how to go about the task of digging a proper hole, one that would be deep enough to keep scavengers from disturbing the cat's resting place. While it was distressing, it gave her something to focus her grief on. It anchored her to something and reeled her in from her sea of helplessness.

As he got up, he said, "I wouldn't take too long; the day's heating up." The binary advice added more weight to the anchor of dread, but disallowed procrastination.

What her family didn't know was that Bailey had not died alone. In the hours leading up to her last breath, Bailey had been joined by a presence. It was one which she sensed as something unknown, but much like the love and warmth and comfort she had felt throughout her lifetime with her people. The presence stroked her face the way she had always loved, until she fell asleep. As she fell deeper, the presence caressed her from neck to tail in soft, lingering strokes. Only Bailey could hear the subdued whispers of peace. She fell asleep purring, and she simply didn't wake up.

TEN

Outside, the cacophony of cicadas could not be ignored. The creatures, now numbering in the hundreds, rattled the hot days away, chasing off hungry birds while trying to attract mates. The cicadas' master plan was to multiply and force every Oklahoman to surrender and adapt to the summer's seasonal tinnitus, talking over the buzz and at times having to repeat yourself if you were near a bank of trees numbering more than three.

Hazel carefully selected a burial plot, the heat of the midsummer day directing her to a small, heavily shaded clearing on the front side of the house. The spot could be viewed by Hazel's favorite reading nook on the stair landing. Hazel liked the idea of being able to see where Bailey lay, and for this reason she decided it would be perfect. The spot would allow them all a chance to acknowledge their bond from two separate planes.

Holden didn't appreciate leaving the cool cave of his room for such a morbid task, but he owed it to Bailey and couldn't think of a better alternative for dealing with what he referred to as her earthly remains.

The shade protected them from the searing sun but provided no abatement from the drone of the cicadas, and the twins were submerged in clingy air. Before long, they gave up on conversation and focused their waning energy on digging, both glad they were not in view of the pool as its cool water oasis would have tempted them to drop their shovels and dive in, shoes and all. The earth was more sodden than the air, making the removal of the red dirt easy.

After agreeing the job was complete, they returned their shovels to the garage, where they found Mom wrapping the box in stretch wrap left over from their move.

"You two are a mess," she said, stating the obvious. "Grab yourselves some water bottles and clean up a bit while I get your dad. Don't go past the laundry room unless you take off those shoes."

The jolt of air-conditioned air gave the twins chills as they rid themselves of their muddy chore sneakers and slipped on their slides. The evaporating sweat left a shell on their bodies, and again, thoughts of jumping in the pool sprang to the front of their minds.

Dad entered the laundry room, distracted by the phone in his hand. He looked up, reset his focus, and silenced his phone, tucking it in his pocket. In the garage, he picked up the box and led the small procession to the site, where he gently placed the box in the hole and covered it with loose rocks. He and Holden took turns shoveling dirt back into the hole, while Hazel and Mom stood arm-in-arm, not hiding their tears.

Dad smoothed out the earth, leaned his shovel against a tree and spoke. "This is a very sad day for our family. But let's remember how lucky we were to have such a great cat. Bailey picked us," he said, pulling Mom close. "When your Mom and I went to adopt a cat, we almost walked right past her. We were looking for a kitten, but she knew we needed her. She reached through the cage and grabbed me, even put several holes in my favorite T-shirt."

Mom smiled as the memory flooded her mind. "We decided she was the one while we pried her claws out of your dad's shirt. She adopted Phineas as her unofficial offspring the day we brought him home. She was his mom, whether he wanted a new mom or not. He hated how she held him down and cleaned him every morning."

They had all heard the stories dozens of times, but the solemn reflection was needed. It felt odd turning their backs on the grave site and leaving Bailey outside, alone. Unlike most of her kin, she had never been fond of the outdoors once she was introduced to the good life inside a house.

Phineas and Coraline had watched the funeral from the cathedral window and as the family entered the house, they were greeted with the same exuberance they would have had they been gone for days.

"I've got a few more things I need to wrap up with work before calling it a day," Dad said. "Thanks for taking such good care of Bailey, Haze. Pass the word on to your brother if you see him."

Holden had already retreated to his room.

Hazel gave a weak nod and slowly climbed the stairs. Coraline followed in her footsteps. The weight of the loss pulled Hazel down, and she wished more than ever that she could escape the confines of the property, to become immersed in anything outside the walls that might take her mind off her heartache.

That night after dinner, Mom brought her laptop to the kitchen island where they sat. "I was thinking of ordering this garden stone, like a memorial marker for Bailey," she said, opening the device. She had chosen their favorite picture of Bailey, one taken when she was younger. The cat was perched in a window, and a beam of light created an aura around her as she basked in its glow. Seeing the image on Mom's laptop caused tears to spill from Hazel's eyes. On the stone would be the words, *Bailey, thank you for the happiness you gave us.*

Hazel was relieved when Dad replied, "It's perfect." She was unable to speak, overcome again with emotion.

Dad suggested watching a comedy to lighten the mood. It was a respectable effort, but it fell flat with the glum group. The twins took the dogs on their nightly outing, and afterward Hazel went to the laundry room out of habit. Her heart sank when remembered she no longer had an ailing cat to tend to.

She saw Mom had removed the litter box and tiny two-sided dish, the cat's only worldly possessions. The absence of the items drained her further; the emptiness grew heavier. How empty could one become? What would be the source that brought fullness back? Perhaps it was simply the passage of time. She knew it was only the first day, but she wondered how many more days she would feel the pain of losing her sweet cat so strongly.

Aching, tired, and vacant, she left the laundry room and drifted through the house on the way to her bedroom. As she approached the foot of the stairs, she heard the familiar beeping noise. It sounded distant from where she stood. She lifted a foot to place it on the first tread when the stomping began. The unseen runner moved quickly, closing in on her. Hazel couldn't form thoughts fast enough as the runner gained new dimension, previously only heard, but now *felt*. She succumbed to the experience as the deafening noise drew nearer. The sound moved through her, her long hair blown back by an invisible force. The atmosphere shivered with an electrical chill and her flesh turned cold, tiny hairs standing on end. For an instant, an earthy bouquet overwhelmed the space. It was a familiar scent, but it took a moment for its complexity to speak to her nose.

Rain, but more than rain. It was the way a person smells after coming in from the rain with soaked hair and drenched clothing, the staleness of moisture as it dampened a person's essence.

As quickly as it had started, it was over. The instability dissipated and the quality of the space normalized, smell faded and flesh smoothed. The effect was dizzying, and she lowered herself to sit on the bottom step. She saw Coraline, huddled in a corner of the farthest reach of the foyer, helpless to defend her owner but unwilling to abandon her. The pup had had an accident, her first in weeks.

Over the dog's whimper, Alexa spoke. "Motion detected at the garage door." The AI's announcement offered no resolution, but signaled the anticipated end of the turbulence. She cleaned up the dog's mess and cautiously climbed the stairs.

As she readied herself for sleep, her reflection struck her as aged, like too much time had passed and etched its forward motion on her young face. She lifted a hand to her darkened eyes, dabbing the swollen swaths below them with gentle fingers.

In her bed, her mind fought to untangle multiple strings of logic as she replayed the occurrence on the stairs and considered Bailey's deathly posture. The roiling images lost focus as the embrace of the cool sheets and soft mattress soothed her sore muscles and muddled mind.

Sleepily, she said, "Alexa, play Sleep Sounds." Her leaden consciousness took no notice that this rendering of Sleep Sounds was actually the dreamy intro of "Memories Fade," and she was asleep before the song's anguished lyrics began. The tune was followed by "Mad World," and the two songs leapfrogged each other while Hazel fell deeper into troubled sleep, only ceasing forty-five minutes later when the predetermined timer expired.

ELEVEN

The sun shone bright through the window, forcing Hazel to rouse from a sleep that was anything but peaceful. She lay in bed and her mind replayed the confusing scenes from the nightmare that had deprived her of rest. Her heart raced as flashes of the bad dream flooded her mind. There was a hole, much larger and deeper than the one she and Holden dug the day before; and a violent storm. All of these troubling images faded away as she opened her eyes; in their place, thoughts of Bailey. Knowing she would never again be greeted by the cat urging Hazel to fill her bowl with the tuna-flavored mush that turned Hazel's stomach.

Coraline granted her a few moments of reprieve before she eagerly pawed at Hazel's arm, insisting her owner get up and let her outside. With a groan, Hazel complied. Departing from their usual routine, Hazel exited the front door. The dog trailed behind, voraciously inhaling the smells of the outside air. Hazel wanted to check on Bailey, and make sure the cat had been left in peace, that nothing had disturbed the fresh grave. As she approached the spot, she stopped so abruptly that Coraline collided with the back of her legs and almost caused her to topple over onto the broken ground. No scavengers had disturbed the plot, but there was a jarring change. Atop the mound were small stones laid out to form the letter *B*. Bundles of wildflowers wilted in the morning sun, encircling the pebbles.

She revolved where she stood, scanning her surroundings, certain she would spy the person who had arranged this memorial. Who would have done this? They knew no one in the neighborhood. She felt increasingly uncomfortable and vulnerable outside, even with the protective dog who was now sniffing around the mound curiously. Hazel turned and sprinted back to the house, calling for Coraline as she ran.

She rushed the dog inside ahead of her, then slammed the door, falling against it, out of breath more from fright than from the short dash. Holden was descending the stairs, hair disheveled, yawning.

"Go for a morning jog? Ambitious, but you might want to rethink your wardrobe choices next time, just saying," he said, noting her attire. She was still in her usual pajama ensemble of sleep shorts and T-shirt, and a robe that was really too small for her, having only slipped her slides on before going outside.

While she was certain the headstone was not his style, she asked, "Did you lay flowers and um, other stuff on Bailey's grave?"

As he left her in the foyer, making his way to the kitchen, he said, "Um, no. What is the traditional gift of mourning for a cat, anyway? Catnip? Sorry, I haven't gotten around to ordering any." He turned to look at her before escaping her line of sight. "My bad."

She didn't appreciate his sarcasm. She was shocked that he could crack jokes so soon, but she knew he wasn't responsible for the memorial. Pulling her phone from her robe pocket, she scrolled until she found the Ring app. She opened the screen and swiped back, stopping at 1 o'clock the previous day and hoping the grave was in view of the camera. She saw the four of them entering the house after Bailey's service, but was discouraged to see the plot was just out of the camera's scope. She hit play, believing whoever had gone through the effort to craft the heartfelt remembrance would likely come into the camera's line of sight during the process. The footage zoomed by uninterrupted, but at 3:14 a.m., a motion indicator popped up and the playback slowed to normal speed. Watching intently, she held her breath and waited for the memorial-laying prowler to show up. The flurry of nightly bugs was rendered invisible as a flash of bright light oversaturated the recording. When the flash burned out, the frenzy of winged pests was gone. The replay sped up again, and she swiped back for a repeat of the only motion captured that night. Anticipating the flash of light, she focused on the aftermath. There was no person, but she did see a distortion, and a haziness materialized at the edge of the camera's scope. Like the fog her Dad insisted was the only thing that could be seen when the garage door sensor chimed. She rewound the footage again, and she recalled something her Dad said about the garage door alert. "It's like a camera flash, then a fog drifts by."

Hazel continued to watch the footage as it sped toward sunrise, and she saw herself emerge from the door, Coraline on her heels. It didn't make sense. For someone to avoid the camera, they would have to approach from the woods and complete the undertaking. It would be much easier and safer to use the driveway. And what was that mist? It wasn't actual fog. It was much too ethereal and seemed to move with purpose rather than roll in to blanket an area.

There was a childish quality to the memorial. Who let their children out in the woods after dark? If it were a group of children, they would have been hard-pressed to avoid the camera's eye.

Mom interrupted her investigation as she came down the stairs and asked, "What are you up to this morning?"

Hazel grabbed Mom's wrist. "You have to come see this," she said, dragging her toward the door.

"Haze, I'm in my pajamas!"

"No one is going to see you out here." Hazel held on to Mom's wrist the whole way, leading her to the spot where they buried the cat.

Mom stood over the fresh grave for a minute. Finally, she asked, "Did you make this? Because I already ordered that stone. It shouldn't take too long to get—"

Hazel cut her off. "No, no, Mom, I *did not* make this! I was trying to find out who did on the Ring, but I couldn't see anyone."

Mom looked around the isolated grounds. "Okay, well that's really weird," she said, glancing at Hazel. Shifting her gaze back to the mound with its cryptic stone *B* and collection of shriveled wildflowers, she shrugged. "Well, if you didn't catch the weirdo on camera, then we'll probably never know who did it. Pretty creepy. I need coffee." Again, she resigned herself to acceptance with no rational explanation.

She paused a moment longer and said, "I miss her already," before she turned and walked away. When she reached the door, she yelled back to Hazel, "It's gonna be another scorcher. Meet me in the pool in an hour or so, okay? And try to talk your brother into joining us."

Hazel remained at the grave, still trying to come up with a realistic scenario. She thought about the way the cat's body had been found. And now this. The ground was bare when the family left it after their informal service—there was no way the display could have spontaneously appeared on its own. A chill shook her as she recalled an article she'd read about a person living in a family's attic while the family blindly accepted things like missing food or misplaced objects. It was called phrogging. She and Miren had watched a horror movie about it. Mom and Dad would laugh if she suggested they scour the house, searching the attic and all the closets to make sure they didn't have a stowaway in their home.

She really couldn't come up with a sensible answer. She hadn't just heard the person running down the stairs last night; she also sensed them. She did not, however, see a person. She decided she wanted to learn more about this house Mom and Dad had chosen as their forever home.

Hazel had always enjoyed a good ghost story; she didn't believe the house was haunted. Besides, the house wasn't that old. It was common knowledge a house should be hundreds of years old to be truly haunted. Despite its ancient appearance, this house wasn't even forty years old.

The presence witnessed the two discover the memorial and was frustrated by their unquestioning acceptance. Of course, the goal had not been to further its desperate plight. It was done out of respect and love for the animal. But it realized it would have to push harder, devise methods that might force the family to understand it needed help. It stood over the grave of the cat it had known for a short time with sadness in its soul for a moment longer before moving into the forest to bide its time.

TWELVE

Gone were the days when boredom with the same old meals could be busted by a sit-down at a favorite restaurant or a quick roll through a drive-thru. On this occasion, Mom used the excuse of a sunburn after foolishly forgetting to use sunscreen to order in, again. Dad couldn't find tip money in the usual spots they left cash lying around. He scanned the foyer table, the kitchen island, the bookshelves in the family room, and came up empty-handed.

"You still making an ATM stop on grocery pick-up day?" he asked Mom.

"Yeah," she replied. "I put fifty on the family room bookshelf yesterday. We should come up with a better place to keep it. I'm bad about just setting it wherever. You check the bookshelf. I'll check my purse."

Mom only had a five in her handbag, and there was no money on the bookshelf. Dad went to his wallet, certain he would have some spare cash. As he did so, he marveled at how long it had been since he had actually placed his wallet in his back pocket, much less taken it out and used it. That daily habit had been abandoned since they were stuck at home. He was disappointed to only find a couple of ones in his wallet, not nearly enough for an adequate tip.

"I know I saw a couple of bills on the entry table a few days ago. At least I thought I did," Mom said, retracing Dad's steps and searching in all the same spots he had looked, peering behind the table and searching the floor.

Not satisfied with the paltry amount and growing frustrated, Dad pounded on Holden's door. Without waiting for a reply, he entered the room. "Hey, son. Have you been helping yourself to the tip money?"

"Cash has lost all use for me, Dad. I literally have not set foot off this property since we moved in," Holden quipped.

Losing patience, Dad moved on to Hazel's bedroom. She had already stepped into the hallway after hearing the harsh tone in his voice.

"I haven't seen the cash, but I've got some birthday money you can have." Hazel handed over two twenty-dollar bills.

"Thanks, Haze," Dad said, taking the money. "I'll pay you back as soon as the missing funds show up."

Over dinner, Dad continued to fume about the misplaced money. Hazel decided this was the perfect time to suggest a search of the house—not for cash, but for someone who had taken it.

"So, I was thinking, with all the weird things happening around here, maybe we should search the house. This might sound insane, but what if someone is living here ... like a squatter or something? Maybe someone is living in the attic." As soon as the words escaped her lips, she realized how paranoid and weird she sounded.

Dad was quiet. Mom was the first to respond. "That's ridiculous. We would absolutely know if someone was lurking about in our attic. How would they use the bathroom? No food has gone missing. Sorry, Haze, but that's a stretch."

Finally, Dad spoke up. "It does seem far-fetched, but having a look around can't hurt."

"I'm sitting this one out," Mom said, as Dad went over the obvious mechanics of only walking on crossbeams and not putting full weight on plywood.

"You better be careful!" Mom admonished. "The last thing we need is for one of you to end up in the emergency room with a broken bone, or worse. I've seen what the hospitals look like. They are overwhelmed, full of people with the virus."

"We'll be extra careful," Dad told her as he checked his flashlight and led the twins upstairs.

Outside the future theater room door, Dad pulled the ladder down that led to the attic. The three realized the stranger living in the attic theory could be debunked right then and there. A large dust cloud blasted their faces as the ladder unfolded. At the same time, the ear-splitting cry from the springs provided definitive evidence. A musty scent escaped the dark, rectangular entrance. It would be impossible for anyone to pass to and from this point without all of them being aware of it. Holden gave the small search party a look that said what they were all thinking.

"Let's go up and see if maybe there's some other access point, just to make one hundred percent sure," Dad said.

When all three had climbed the ladder and gathered in the stale space, Dad found a bare light fixture and was surprised to discover the bulb still had life. In the waning light, they could see that the space was enormous but empty, aside from an ancient antenna that spanned an inordinate amount of space. "Now that I think about it, I'm sure Dave would have let us know if there was evidence of human vermin living up here."

"To be fair, you asked the man to search for squirrels and

raccoon; there was no obligation to tell you about human life. Plus, if the boogeyman in the attic is the same person who gets his cardio on the staircase every night, well, he's a speedy dude. Anyone who can make it back up here as fast as him would have no trouble using his elite abilities to hide from the Critter Getter," Holden said, looking at his twin, his expression betraying his annoyance, his tone leaving zero doubt.

Feeling foolish for even suggesting someone would have been living in the attic, Hazel began her backward climb down the ladder. "Sorry. Waste of time. Dumb theory."

"Nothing ventured!" Dad called down.

Holden mumbled, punctuating key words under his breath, "Lame! Waste of time!"

Dad swept the beam of his flashlight through the vast space, finding nothing out of the ordinary and, most convincingly, no other visible point of entry. He pulled the grimy string to extinguish the unnatural light before climbing down. The harsh cry of the springs underlined their failure.

Hazel and Holden were prepping to take the dogs out when they heard Mom's gasp followed by the sound of smashing glass. The twins rushed toward the noise.

In the dining room Mom stood, her bare feet surrounded by shards from a shattered wine glass that had slipped from her hand, and was forgotten about when she saw a jar in the china hutch. Inside a Ball Mason drinking mug were all denominations of paper money, neatly folded. The bottom of the cup was filled with loose change.

Dad entered the room from the opposite direction. He first saw the broken glass; then his eyes drifted to Mom's face, down her outstretched arm, past the tip of her extended finger.

"I don't know which one of you thought this stunt might be funny," he bellowed. "We will talk about this tomorrow. For now, get the dogs out and get ready for bed while I help Mom clean this mess up," he instructed with finality.

Mom heard her children laughing as she descended the stairs the next morning. She found Hazel and Holden hovering over cereal bowls staring intently at a viral video, eating paused for a moment of particular amusement.

Before she could speak, Holden started in. "Mom, I swear, it wasn't me! I wouldn't do anything like that. It wasn't even funny!" He pleaded his defense and pardoned himself at once.

Hazel angrily, but internally, applauded his straightforward approach, establishing innocence while simultaneously throwing her under the bus. Well played. She glanced at him, her face expressing a mixture of awe, anger, envy, acceptance.

"Don't look at me!" Hazel chimed in. "Look, Mom, we don't know how the money got there, but it wasn't us."

Mom looked at her children. She knew their tells, and could sense their sincerity. She believed their propensity for honesty far outweighed their ability to lie, and knew they were being truthful.

Holden didn't think Mom was convinced, so he pressed on. "Come on, Mom. Think about the things that have happened. The noises on the stairs, the disembodied alarm at the garage door, the way Bailey was found, the creepy setup on her grave. Something strange is going on. How much weirder is it for money to show up in a jar?"

"It's absurd, but consistent," Mom agreed.

"No more absurd than all the other stuff, really," he replied.

That statement gave her pause before she redirected her attention to Hazel. "So, what are you suggesting? We have a ghost? Is that what you think, Hazel?"

Hazel shot Holden another look, this one imparting shock, confusion, and disadvantage. "I don't know, Mom. All we are saying is we didn't put the money in the jar. Why would we lie about something so lame?"

"Well, hopefully your father will have forgotten it today. What else could this house have in store? None of it makes any sense. It's not as if we can just pop over to the neighbors and ask about any of it." Her words were delivered in a choppy, rapid-fire style. She paced the room, twirling a ringlet of her hair around and around her finger in perpetual motion.

As if the virus wasn't enough to stress anyone out, things weren't getting better in the world. Quarantine fatigue was setting in. The end of the pandemic loomed before them, months, maybe years away, the experts warned. Add to it the strange, unexplained occurrences inside their bubble where all was supposed to be safe, and it took stress to a whole other level. Hazel got up and gave her mom a hug.

Holden joined in, wrapping his long arms around them both. "I'm getting in on this hug-fest. Don't worry. It isn't a real problem until the house starts saying, 'Get out!' or the walls start bleeding."

THIRTEEN

Hazel set about to learn what she could about the house and its former occupants, certain there had to be a nugget of information online that might answer some questions. After all, the internet knew everything. She coerced Mom into assisting in her cause by having her email the president of the Homeowners Association. Mom was beyond reluctant, not wanting to come off as seeming crazy. In the end, all she could commit to was requesting a copy of the neighborhood directory and making a few random inquiries.

Hazel believed the vague and broad quality of Mom's questions rendered the whole effort pointless. She didn't share her feelings with Mom, as she knew she was already stretching far beyond her comfort zone.

Coincidentally, the same day the two rookie sleuths began their investigation, the Weizaks had their first visitor at the Shrek house. Late in the morning, Alexa unexpectedly announced, "Motion detected at the front door." The report was followed by the electronic chime of the doorbell. This drew everyone but Holden away from their current preoccupations.

There was a constant flow of packages delivered to the house, setting off a front door alert once or twice a day. Alexa would announce motion, but the arrival had already been given away by the lumbering of a truck easing over the bridge. Sometimes the driver would rap gently on the door, but they never rang the bell.

A ringing doorbell used to be a standard event but now felt ominous, almost dangerous. If the fear in the air weren't so palpable, the family's reaction to something so reasonable would have been humorous.

Mom was thrown off her game. She didn't ask Alexa to show her who was at the front door. Instead, she quickly made her way to the entryway where she met Dad. He slowly approached the door, Mom behind him, clutching the back of his shirt as if they were facing down a masked intruder in the dark of night. In actuality, they were answering their door in the middle of a radiant day in a safe, secluded neighborhood. Dad even used the ridiculous hatch in the door, arguably the world's most conspicuous peephole, to check to see who stood outside their home. Upon opening the medieval aperture, Dad let out a discernible sigh of relief, coupled with a chuckle. Mom relaxed a bit, and choked out a nervous laugh too as Dad closed the hatch, slid the locking mechanism and opened the door to the least intimidating visitor one could imagine.

"Good morning, neighbors! My name is Lula Clarkson. I live next door," she said. She held a small package in her hands. Her full face was exposed. "My apologies for not wearing a mask. I promise to keep my distance. I forget the darn thing all the time. This virus has robbed me of my manners too. I'm not sure I'll ever get used to not extending a hand upon meeting new friends."

Mom and Dad stumbled over words, both apologetic and empathetic.

Hazel listened from the stairway landing where she had corralled the dogs, embarrassed for her parents.

"I used to welcome new neighbors with a plate of my oatmeal cookies, but these days it seems everyone is allergic to something, so I gave up on that. But I didn't come empty-handed," she said, handing over the package. "The carrier delivered this to my house by mistake. It belongs to you, Mr. Weizak. Is that how it is pronounced?"

Her words came out quickly and boldly and without the slightest bit of hesitation. She couldn't have been more than five feet tall, even taking into account the slight hunch of her posture. A long, thick braid of white hair draped over her shoulder, strands escaping in a halo around her face. Her skin was the color of rose rock, and she wore thick, round glasses that seemed far too large for her petite face. Perhaps their bright purple hue made them seem bigger than they actually were. She had draped herself in turquoise jewelry in a myriad of shades ... rings, bracelets, necklaces of varying lengths and large, dangling earrings that drooped so heavily, they looked as if they would be painful. An oversized denim sundress swallowed up her tiny frame, and sand-colored Birkenstocks completed her look.

They transitioned outside, away from the airless interior of the house, to where the circulation of fresh air seemed safest. Mom and Dad made an awkward show of hosting a surprise guest while social distancing.

Hazel scrambled up the stairs to the spare bedroom which now housed their home gym equipment. The room was an oddity among oddities in this house. It held its own bathroom and washer and dryer. Its window sat directly above the front porch. She slid the window up silently, stifling a cough as the heat of the outside pushed its way in to her face, and listened to the conversation below.

"You folks settling in nicely? I noticed your Colorado plates. Don't think you could have picked a worse time to move now, could ya?" she said with a chuckle.

"It certainly wasn't ideal, but the ball had been rolling before the virus crisis. We've hopped around a bit, this time from Colorado. But this is where we are putting down roots and hanging up our hats," Dad told Mrs. Clarkson, who insisted on being called Lula.

"I've lived in Stillwater my whole life. My husband, Roy, five years passed, rest his soul, built out here in Camelot Crossing when we were almost empty nesters. Our two daughters moved onto campus while attending the university, so they weren't too far."

Hearing she had lived in the neighborhood since it had first become a neighborhood, Hazel crouched below the window in the upstairs room and silently willed Mom to ask prying questions, hoping against hope Mom would go out on a limb and find out what she could about the house they resided in. It was apparent the pandemic isolation had worn on Lula, and she was grateful to have people to talk to. How lonely living alone during this time would be. Finally, Hazel heard her Mom say the words she had hoped she would. In a tentative tone, Mom asked, "So if you've lived here since the beginning, you must know a lot about the neighborhood?"

Hazel whispered, "Go, Mom!" and leaned closer to the window.

"Well, I do think I've known just about everyone who has come and gone from this neighborhood over the years. I am the chairman of the Welcoming Committee, after all," she replied. "Back in the day I used to welcome the newcomers and recommend butchers, tire stores, hair salons, you know, those kinds of things. These days nobody needs that stuff. The internet can tell you all you need to know in a few clicks. So mostly I am responsible for providing people with the neighborhood directory."

"That's funny; I emailed the HOA president requesting the directory just this morning," Mom said with an ironic laugh.

"Oh dear. Well, I hope he doesn't fire me for shirking my duties." She paused in anticipation of laughter, and Mom and Dad obliged after skipping a beat. "I will put one in your mailbox tomorrow," she went on to say.

Mom thanked her and segued into her next question with a smoothness that impressed Hazel. "Since you are the one in the know, you must know a great deal about the history of this house. The past residents and such," she said, striking the perfect balance of inquiry and flattery, not too awkward considering the awkward nature of the transition. This question seemed to give Lula pause, which intrigued Hazel.

For the first time during the conversation, she was lost for words and unsure how to proceed. After a moment, she gathered her thoughts and said, "This house has seen more families than any other house in the neighborhood. People never seem to stay here too long for one reason or another."

Although Hazel couldn't see Mom's face from her position, she could picture her mom's expression as she pressed Lula to continue.

"Really?" Mom questioned. Her eyes widened as she nudged Dad. She was certain this was some important piece of the puzzle; subtlety was never one of Mom's strong suits.

Hazel did have to admit it was an interesting tidbit, but on its own wasn't all that telling. She hoped one of them would push for more details, but neither had to.

Lula continued to recount the former inhabitants one by one, beginning with the man who built the house. He had been a professional golfer. The mansion's walls shrunk as rapidly as his rankings and bank account grew. His status demanded a grander house than the massive Tudor. At this point the house slipped into its first hibernation, one of many.

"The house sat empty for a time. No offense, it is a bit unusual. It takes a person with certain tastes to see the beauty in a house like this," Lula said, vastly understating the obvious.

"It certainly is unique," Dad agreed, not at all offended by the woman's bluntness.

"It changed hands many times after that. I'd say no family ever stayed here more than two or three years. I remember because I brought more Welcome Wagon packages to this house than to any other. Must've brought dozens of cookies through this door. There was a dean at the college, and a coach of the Cowgirl Softball team, I recall. And then a doctor, maybe. I was never really close with any of them.

"At the turn of the century, the house had its longest occupants," Lula continued. From above, Hazel turned this statement over in her mind a few times. She'd never heard anyone describe the year 2000 as "turn of the century." She wandered away from the conversation for a moment, mulling the phrase over.

"They owned a restaurant in town and were rather successful. I believe they gave birth to a son while they lived here. They owned the place for about five years, but their business fell on hard times and the house went into foreclosure. Yes, I think they were the longest owners. Once they left, the house sat empty. You're probably aware it was vacant for almost two years before you came along."

Lula had obviously reached the end of the parade of Shrek house inhabitants. Hazel tried to ignore the pins and needles in her legs and held her breath, waiting for Mom to ask the next most obvious question.

Very casually Mom said, "So, do you know if anyone died in the house?"

Lula reclaimed that quick, assured tone and replied, "Oh no, dear. I can assure you no one has ever died in the house."

FOURTEEN

Most would take comfort in learning there had been no deaths in their home, but it was almost a letdown. They wanted something easy on which to place blame and that would explain all the strange events. Somehow, saying a ghost was responsible would be an easy and acceptable explanation, no matter how preposterous. No one really believed in ghosts anymore. They were the things of childhood nightmares and fodder for television channels that claimed to be sources of learning. Ghosts were lore that gave you the creeps around Halloween and made slumber parties more entertaining. They weren't something used to explain weird things happening in your home.

Hazel decided the best thing to do would be to push the events out of her mind and ignore all of it. If no one had died in the house, how could it possibly be haunted? She was going to give up on her research, which hadn't amounted to much. Nothing pertaining to the house itself had come up, just a bit about the golfer. Mom seemed content knowing no one had actually died inside the home. But she quantified her relief with the acknowledgment that most people probably had no idea about deaths that had taken place in their dwellings.

"The person who lived in our Colorado home passed away there, in her sleep," Mom told them at dinner that night. "Nothing weird ever happened after that."

Holden detached himself from his phone. "You've kept this from us all this time? I would've dusted off the Ouija board if I'd known. Dude, bro, dude ... did you hear that?" Only Hazel got the reference to one of Holden's favorite TV shows from when he was eight. Mom gave him "the look," which he didn't notice because before he was done speaking; his focus was back on his phone.

With this new information, they decided to just accept things and move on. What choice did they have, really? It seemed doable. There was enough craziness in the world to worry about without stressing about bizarre things taking place in their home. The virus was not letting up. The claims that warmer weather would slow the spread were proving false. They couldn't let their house turn on them. It was supposed to be their sanctuary.

Unfortunately, the presence still needed to be heard. Time was running out. It was done biding its time. It had spent many years being ignored by the many inhabitants of the house who were too busy to notice or too blind to see its pleas. But things were happening not far from the house that made the situation urgent, and so the presence could not slip quietly into the woods to await another group of people whom it would try to reach out to. While the house sat vacant, it had gathered its strength and devised new ways to make itself known. Now it would stop at nothing, so its secrets could be revealed. The presence wished no harm to anyone. It yearned for other ways to manifest its goals, but in its given state, options were limited.

It needed resolution for the ones it loved and decisively set about to do so.

74   LISA COURTAWAY

It needed resolution for the ones it loved and decisively set about to do so.

FIFTEEN

The day after their first neighborly visit, resolute in her plan to ignore the strange events, Hazel decided to tackle a dreaded task—removing the wallpaper in her room. After watching eighty-four (or three) YouTube videos, she considered herself well-informed and up for the job. She gathered the tools she needed: a spray bottle containing a mixture of liquid fabric softener and hot water, a large putty knife, gloves, and a step ladder. Tying her hair up in a bandanna, she asked Alexa to play her Favorites Playlist.

The paper had bubbled and peeled in some spots, which helped make the work easier. She started in a corner that was peeling badly and was able to discard the putty knife, as the paper lifted off easily. She was glad that it was going well, as she had envisioned the typical DIY process being made more complicated by the virus. She had feared it would snowball and require Mom and Dad's involvement, tears of frustration, and multiple trips to the curbside pickup lane at the hardware store. Excited that things were moving along so well and focused on the music, she didn't pay attention to what was being revealed underneath the wallpaper.

Soon the outdated wallpaper was gone, and she admired her work. It was then that she noticed a faint, repetitive pattern discernible over all three walls. She stepped as far back from one of the walls as she could in an effort to make sense of the markings. From there she saw the letters more clearly. They read,   *HELPLAURACOMBSHELPLAURACOMBSHEL*. There were no spaces between the letters, so it took a moment to realize what it really said, *HELP LAURA COMBS*.

Hazel dropped the last remnants of wallpaper that she had wadded up in a ball, and bolted from her room, looking for someone, anyone, to confirm to her what she was seeing. While her focus had been on deciphering the writing on the wall, she hadn't noticed Alexa had slipped "Memories Fade" into her playlist.

While Hazel was attempting to make out the message on her walls, Mom was in the kitchen baking brownies, partly out of boredom, partly out of craving chocolate, and partly out of the worldwide phenomena of pandemic baking. Alone in the kitchen, she relied on Alexa to keep her company as well as refresh her memory on the amount of butter and cocoa she needed.

As she went about mixing ingredients, she said, "Alexa, tell me three things I need to know." The disembodied AI usually shared newsworthy topics that weren't too alarming and in doing so Mom felt in touch, but not overwhelmed, by the world's chaos.

Today the device started off by stating, "On April 9th, 1984, in Stillwater, Oklahoma, a thirteen-year-old girl named Laura Combs disappeared from her bedroom in the home she shared with her mother. Laura wasn't reported missing until the following day. Organized search parties did not begin searching for Laura until she had been missing for several days as authorities believed she was a runaway. Aerial searches were done, and divers searched local ponds and lakes. Authorities abandoned the search when her mother's live-in boyfriend provided details suggesting the child left on her own. Laura's mother denied these claims and has continued to search for her daughter via grassroots efforts. To this day Laura Combs remains listed as missing with the National Center for Missing and Exploited Children, as neither she nor her remains have ever been located."

The words *Stillwater, Oklahoma* caught Mom's attention, and she paused, one hand holding a pan of uncooked brownies, the other on the handle of the upper oven, to listen to the story. She was distracted by hearing such a random, non-topical report, as she placed the pan in the oven. Alexa did not have a chance to proceed to the second thing she needed to know before Hazel rushed into the room, out of breath and looking panicked. She dropped onto one of the bar stools and splayed her upper body out across the island. Mom readied herself for an update about Miren or a new boyfriend, but then quickly remembered new boyfriends were hard to come by in quarantine.

Mom wanted to share the story the AI had just told her, but waited as Hazel managed to gasp out the directive, "You've got to come upstairs and see this! You aren't going to believe it!" Hazel hopped off the bar stool and grabbed Mom's wrist, dragging her in the direction of the stairs. Mom feared that Hazel had done something during her wallpaper removal to cause horrible damage upstairs. She pushed past her daughter, shaking her off her arm. In the now vacant kitchen, an image came up on the Show. It was a missing poster showing Laura Combs as she appeared the day she disappeared.

Mom braced herself for disaster as she reached the teen's

room. She stopped short, looking for an electrical fire or water spraying from pipes or some other disaster. She moved farther into the room and was impressed by what she saw. Hazel had removed all the wallpaper with very little mess. She had even balled up all the remnants into a nice, tidy bundle. Rushing behind her, still breathless, Hazel pointed frantically.

"Okay drama-mama, yes, I see! You did a great job! It looks amazing!" her mom said in an effort to placate her daughter and hopefully calm the hyped-up teenager.

"No! Look! Look at the walls!" Hazel exclaimed. "The words!"

Hazel could tell Mom wasn't making out the pattern, so she traced over them with her fingers.

As Hazel continued to point out the letters, Mom could see the message, and the letters almost seemed to grow more prominent as her mind accepted what it was seeing.

Hazel continued down the wall. "Help, Laura, Combs," she said as drew over the letters that repeated over and over, wrapping around and proceeding again in another row, equally spaced. It looked as if someone had dipped a finger in paint and written in the words in broad strokes. The effect was dizzying, and Hazel was now certain the words were becoming darker, their insistence growing.

She was relieved that Mom could see the message she was seeing. She bent over, hands on her knees, attempting to catch her breath. Mom was slowly walking back and forth eyeing the walls from every angle when Dad entered the room without looking up from his phone.

"Smells like something is burning," he said distractedly. That got Mom's attention. She hadn't set a timer for the brownies! She turned, rushing out of the room in a desperate attempt to save them.

Hazel waved Dad over. "Look, look! Do you see it?"

"Wow, Haze, great job! You're hired. I've got about forty other projects I need you to get started on pronto."

She flapped her hands at him in annoyance. "No, no, look at the walls! Look at the words." She went over the letters again with her finger, tracing the letters out for him, saying them out loud, stopping at the final S. "Help Laura Combs! It says, Help Laura Combs, over and over again on my walls!"

"Yeah, I see that. How odd. I wonder who this Laura person is. My guess is it was some gag the contractors played on each other when they painted."

Mom returned to the room. "I saved the brownies, and I think I might know who this Laura Combs is." She then relayed Alexa's curious story about the missing girl.

SIXTEEN

With a name, date and location, the family gathered around Mom's laptop at the kitchen island. Mom typed, *Laura Combs, April, 9, 1984, Stillwater, OK,* and hit enter. Google returned about 103,000 results. The first one was a story from *The Stillwater News Press* dated April 9, 2019. It was titled, "Where is Laura Combs? Stillwater Girl Still Missing After 35 Years." Mom clicked the link to the story and read the article aloud.

Where Is Laura Combs? Stillwater Girl Still Missing After 35 Years

Ask any of Stillwater's lifelong citizens if they know the name Laura Combs, and the answer will likely be yes. Ask any of them if they care to speculate about what happened to the girl, missing thirty-five years today, and you will hear many different theories. The story of what happened to Laura Combs is one of Stillwater's biggest mysteries. Laura's mother, Charlotte Combs-Childers, has pushed to make sure her daughter's name, face and story are not forgotten. Mrs. Combs-Childers pressured local and state authorities to reopen the case of her missing daughter, never believing the official stance of Stillwater officials who in

1984 closed the case. Their findings were that Laura had simply run away from home.

The case was reopened in 1988, after a new sheriff was elected in Payne County. Sheriff Clarence Reed, who ran uncontested until his retirement in 2004, had this to say about the case: "I was never convinced that Laura Combs was a runaway. The facts made it difficult to wrap your head around. There was virtually no physical evidence, no real motive and not much in the way of leads. The Stillwater Police Department and Payne County Sheriff's Department did what they could at the time with the information they had. However, awareness, advances in law enforcement techniques and quite frankly, gut instinct, made it impossible for me to close the book on the case. It remains open and will remain open, so new leads may be investigated and evidence can be submitted should it be made available."

Laura's mother reported the child missing the morning of April 10th, 1984. The child's bedroom window was found open; her room was in disarray and rain-soaked. Laura's mother was at work at the time of her disappearance. The only person home with the child at the time was the mother's live-in boyfriend, Ronald Wayne "Bubba" Floyd. Laura's mother reported that the girl was wearing a tan Members Only jacket, a hooded sweatshirt with ladybugs on it, blue jeans, yellow rain boots and a Swatch. A flashlight was missing from the girl's room as well.

The search for Laura Combs was hampered by a number of circumstances. No exact timeline could be established. When questioned, Mr. Floyd indicated the child went to her room upon returning home from school, where she stayed for the remainder of the night. Mr. Floyd stated he fell asleep on the couch around 9:30 p.m., where he slept until Laura's mother woke him in the morning.

A heavy thunderstorm hammered the area that night and

well into the early morning hours. Police surmise the rain may have washed away valuable evidence including footprints and trace evidence left by the child and/or anyone she may have left with. Tracking dogs were not deployed by the police at the time. While friends and neighbors began searching as soon as the girl was discovered missing, an organized search was not formed until April 12th, spearheaded and privately funded by Mr. Wallace Childers. Over the next several days an aerial search was implemented, and a canine search and rescue team was brought in to search local ponds and lakes. Mr. Childers and his family started a reward fund. At the time the reward was $10,000. Today the reward fund has grown to $50,000, but it still has not led to any viable leads regarding the whereabouts of Laura Combs.

Mrs. Combs-Childers has never given up hope that she will learn what happened to her daughter, saying, "For many years I hung on to the hope that Laura was out there somewhere, alive. Now that so many years have passed, the hope of finding her alive has faded. I believe if she were alive, she would've come back to me by now. She did not run away. She was a happy child. She loved her life. What I wish for now is to have answers and to have her home with me, so I can give her a proper burial."

Mom pushed back in her chair as if to distance herself from the despair the article conveyed. She waved a hand in front of her face, symbolically erasing the words she read.

"I can't read anymore. It's so sad," she said.

Hazel had listened numbly to the words and fixated on the missing poster that ran alongside the news story. A dated image of a young girl, only slightly younger than herself, but who looked much more childlike in comparison. The missing child was smil-ing. Hazel was struck by the innocent nature of the smile. In the picture, she was wearing a simple polo-style shirt with rainbow stripes and had long, wavy brown hair held back in a clip shaped like a cloud. The girl had a dimple and bright eyes. This image had school picture written all over it, and Hazel realized it was likely the last school picture Laura Combs had ever taken. There was another photo, which was an age-progressed rendering; the kind that never looked quite right. The face was often at an odd angle, or some other key element was left askew in an unnatural way. The photos all apologetically said, *We know this isn't exactly what the person would look like ... but it's pretty close.*

Dad clicked the back button, and they began to look at some of the other Google hits related to their search. There was a link to the National Centers for Missing and Exploited Children labeling Laura Combs as "Endangered Missing." Other links were for The Charley Project, WebSleuths, WikiFind, a Facebook page called Help Find Laura Combs, and more news stories. The enigma had even been featured on the television show "Unsolved Mysteries."

Dad clicked on the images link and multiple photos of missing posters popped up. Some posters included the age-progressed photo; others did not. One showed the articles of clothing Laura was believed to be wearing. There was a photo of Laura Combs's mother from an old newspaper story. She looked eerily similar to Laura's age-progressed image.

That night, Hazel lay in bed mulling over the mystery of Laura Combs. Rolling over onto her side, she saw her clock read 9:59 p.m. and subconsciously braced herself for the anticipated nightly running of the stairs. As expected, the beeping broke the silence, quickly followed by the footfalls. This time, however, the spectral sound stopped short before running down the stairs. Lifting her head off the pillow, Hazel focused her senses on the sound and the rhythm; everything about it had been so ingrained in her mind that the change brought back the fear and confusion of the first night. The runner had stopped on the other side of her door.

Sitting up, she saw motion under the door—the shadow of feet. She threw the covers back and sprinted to the door. As she swung it open, she yelled, "Holden! That's not—"

The words and her breath seized in her throat. Holden was not outside her bedroom. The hallway was empty and dark. A chill set over her. She didn't *feel* like she was alone in the hall. Cloudy puffs of breath pushed out of her gasping lungs. As she exhaled, she heard a sharp inhale, and her breath disappeared as if sucked into a vacuum, stolen right out of the air.

Recalling a TikTok video she had seen of someone claiming they captured an unseen entity using Snapchat filters, she drew out her phone and opened the app, quickly clicking the first filter at the bottom of the screen, which was floppy puppy ears and a snout. Instantly the app recognized an unseen face as the dog filter appeared over the void beyond her doorway. Her breathing quickened and plumes of visible vapor expelled in sharp gasps as the image tilted, an inquisitive nod of an unseen head moving like they were taking in the face before them. Hazel's face.

And then she was alone again. The chill dissipated, leaving an electrical buzz hanging in the air, and the unmistakable smell of rain permeated the space. The app dropped its goofy filter, searching again for a face to frame. She slammed the door and turned to run back to her bed, wishing to throw the covers over her head and hide like a frightened child. As she did so, she tripped. Coraline was low on her haunches, right behind her, a silent snarl making the dog almost unrecognizable.

"Ugh, Coraline!" Hazel stammered, trying to keep herself from falling on top of the dog. Hearing her name, the dog dropped and rolled over, revealing her belly, as if waiting to be petted. The dog's whining belied her need for a belly rub and frightened Hazel even more. Righting herself, she reached for the dog. "Come on, Cora, it's okay." The dog followed her to the bed and jumped up next to her.

None of the Weizaks slept well that night, but for Hazel, the terrifying dreams made it almost impossible. The nightmare roared to life behind her closed eyes shortly after she nodded off. It was vague and surreal, with no real beginning or end. It had an out-of-body feel too. There was water; she was sinking. The water was red and swirling, there were flashes of light and booming, thunderous sounds. The most striking part of the nightmare was the helpless feeling, like there was no hope and all was lost. This time she woke herself from the dream, crying. She could not remember a time when she had awakened from a dream crying. Her sobs awoke Coraline as well. The dog whined and placed a paw on her face in an act of concern. Hazel drew the dog close, but sleep eluded her until the dark sky brightened.

SEVENTEEN

The following day was gloomy. Pop-up storms built and broke off and on as the day passed. Hazel spent the entire morning in her room on her MacBook reading everything she could about Laura Combs. She was surprised at how much information there was, especially since so little was known about what could have happened to the girl so many years ago.

She watched the piece that had aired on "Unsolved Mysteries." The video clip had been uploaded to the Facebook page. The host recounted the scant details in a serious voice, his cadence paced perfectly, setting an ominous tone for the riddle.

As she watched the clip, she was struck by the feeling she had seen the place where Laura Combs had lived. The notion seemed ridiculous since she hadn't been in Stillwater long, and she certainly hadn't had the chance to explore the town. As the host relayed the chilling account, images from Laura's life flashed on the screen. The scene opened on the front gate of a place called Dark Horse Ranch, and panned to a tree trunk wrapped in yellow ribbon that was tied in a bow, and an old mobile home. There was a brief interview with Laura's mother in which she sat on a small bed in a room where posters of horses, kittens, and dogs hung on the wood paneled walls. Footage of Bubba Wallace entering the police station sent a chill up Hazel's spine. His dark eyes glared at the camera, unblinking and angry. Mr. Wallace had promptly left town as soon as the case was closed. There was a photo of the man too. A mugshot that made him look dark and mean.

Unable to shake the nagging feeling of familiarity, Hazel opened a maps app and typed Dark Horse Ranch, Stillwater, OK in the search bar. As the request loaded, she almost dropped her phone. She was shocked to see how close the ranch was to her house. Dark Horse Ranch was less than three miles away by car, but the property lines were much closer. If one were to brave the woods behind the Weizaks' house, they could stumble upon Dark Horse Ranch in no time. The ranch and the Shrek house were, in a sense, neighbors. The map prompted her memory, and she realized where she had seen the Dark Horse Ranch. Anyone heading to Camelot Crossing drove past the gate and its molded iron sign.

She read the write-ups on The Charley Project and theories on WebSleuths and Reddit. She had no idea so many kids went missing every day and tried to avoid being sucked in by the haunting images of hundreds of vanished children. It was appalling and sad and terrifying. Where did they all go? What happened to them? Some profiles contained ample information and details leading authorities to believe the children had been abducted by family members. Hazel had to hope those kids, while in horrible situations and being missed by countless people who loved and cared for them, were safe. Others had barely any information, only scant, sketchy details. No one knew what had happened to those children. It was as if they vanished into thin air. Laura Combs was one of those kids.

Around noon, Mom knocked on her bedroom door and

asked her to come have a bite to eat with her. She had made Hazel's favorite rainy-day lunch—grilled cheese and tomato soup. As the two sat together, Hazel shared what she had learned about the missing girl. She had pored over the Facebook page dedicated to leads and information regarding Laura.

"At first I thought maybe her dad kidnapped her. But he came forward when she disappeared and was cooperative. He even took a lie detector test. His alibi checked out. He was in Vegas when she disappeared."

"Her poor mother. I can't imagine anything worse," Mom commented, pushing her unfinished soup away.

"That's not the worst of it. So many sightings have been reported, still to this day. Most are blatant fabrications. Greedy people, out for the reward money."

"Vultures," Mom said, shaking her head.

"Did you know people try to sell information to families of the missing? Weirdos insisted she had been kidnapped by aliens. Psychics claimed to know where she was buried or being held. Some of them even appeared on talk shows. Obviously, none of their predictions led anywhere. Maybe she was trafficked."

"How dare people try to profit off such a horrific loss," Mom replied, as a tear slid down her cheek.

"She lived really close to here, you know?"

"Did she? How close?" Mom asked.

"Just through the woods behind our house," Hazel told her.

"Shut up!" Mom replied, looking out the window over her shoulder.

"Right? I wonder if someone who built this house knew something."

"Why would you think that?"

"The writing on my bedroom wall. Maybe someone knew something, had a guilty conscious. Or maybe you knew something, or someone involved. You are the only one of us who lived here before."

"Well, that seems like a stretch. I've lain awake at night wondering about it. I don't remember hearing anything when I was in college. But I didn't pay much attention to local news, especially if it wasn't campus related. The names don't sound familiar to me. I barely knew this neighborhood existed."

Hazel noticed Mom's laptop and saw that Mom was doing some research herself. On the screen was an image of the missing poster.

"You know, I think you look a lot like her," said Mom, turning her attention now to her laptop.

"Mmm, no, I don't see it," Hazel said, moving the laptop closer for a better look.

"Maybe we should send her mother a Facebook message," Mom suggested.

"What would we say? 'Hey, Alexa told us about your missing daughter. We have these strange things happening in our house. Thought we'd reach out tell you about it.' She would think we were crazy, no better than the psychics and UFO people."

"True."

The presence knew it would have to summon more strength. It would have to speak louder, find new ways to make itself heard. It could not be silent. It could not be ignored. The presence had watched the family closely and knew who to focus its energy on. The younger girl. She was almost there, almost ready to hear what the presence needed to say.

EIGHTEEN

"I'm reminding you, check the pool." Alexa woke them at midnight. In every room, the devices repeated, "I'm reminding you, check the pool. I'm reminding you, check the pool."

Hazel woke, confused and groggy. Her device seemed to be yelling at her. She commanded, "Alexa, stop!" Her Dot quieted, but she could still hear the unnerving echo blaring loudly through other parts of the house. Coraline jumped off the bed and was barking at her door. Hazel got up and left her bedroom. Mom and Dad were already in the hallway, and Holden exited his room at the same time she did, everyone mumbling questions. Holden had shut his Dot up. Mom was heading for the exercise room to quiet the device housed in that room while Dad headed downstairs to hush the gadgets on the lower level. They were all so loud, they reverberated through the walls.

Dad came back up the stairs slowly, scratching his chest, seemingly still half asleep, but obviously not amused by the rude awakening.

"I don't know which one of you is responsible for this

stunt," he said, "but I don't find it one bit amusing. Tomorrow we will get to the bottom of it, and there will be repercussions. For now, get back to bed. Good night!" He and Mom returned to their bedroom and Dad calmly closed the door behind them.

Holden and Hazel stood in the hallway, looking at each other questioningly, each of them waiting for the other to confess to having executed such a daring but miserable prank. Neither one of them bent, and finally Holden shrugged, turned back to his room, and closed his door.

Hazel stood in the hall a moment longer, feeling anxious. Check the pool. What could that mean? Who had scheduled some middle-of-the-night reminder on all the devices and increased the volume? It didn't seem like anything Holden would have come up with, much less spent the time and effort pulling off.

She felt overwhelmed by it all as she returned to her bed and called Coraline to come up. Too on edge to sleep, she reached for her Kindle to take her mind off things, hoping some light reading would lull her back to sleep. It had been a while since she had used the e-reader. She couldn't remember what she had been reading but was happy to see device still had some battery life. She opened the first listing in her lineup, a poetry book. What appeared on her Kindle was not poetry. The screen was filled with the same message hidden behind her tapestries: *HELP LAURA COMBS, HELP LAURA COMBS.* The words filled the screen like a strobe light, and the message scrolled repeatedly. She pushed the page forward button, hoping the message would disappear. While the plea for help was gone, a new message kept repeating: *CHECK THE POOL. CHECK THE POOL.* She was too unnerved to try another page and tossed the device under her bed without turning it off.

She considered leaving her bedroom light on, like a child

afraid of the dark, but willed herself to get a grip. It took forever to fall asleep again and when she did finally doze off, her dreams were filled with broken images and a sense of dread and despair. This time, however, there was more to the nightmare. She was outside in the thick of a storm and was looking into the woods. As lightning flashed, she could see an outline of a man standing in the tree line. She awoke again, in fear—panic, really —with tears streaming down her face. These nightmares were starting to wear on her. Each night a little more was being revealed, but they still held no context.

Bleary eyed, she rolled over to check the clock. The sun had yet to come up, and her room was still cast in dark shadows. She was surprised to see the time on her Dot was 9:18 a.m. The sun was definitely up. Still reluctant to get out of bed, she grabbed her phone to check the weather, expecting to see another rainy day. But when she opened her weather app, she was surprised to see the forecast indicated sunny skies. Disbelieving her sources and hoping to fall back asleep for a couple of more hours she rolled over, pulled the covers over her head as she asked, "Alexa, what's the weather like?"

Alexa promptly replied, "Currently in Stillwater, Oklahoma, it is eighty degrees Fahrenheit with sunny skies. You can expect plenty of sunshine today with a high temperature of ninety-two degrees Fahrenheit."

Sunny skies? The absence of light in her bedroom did not reflect sunny skies. Reluctantly, she threw the covers back and sat up in bed. She eyeballed the clock on her Dot and compared it to her phone. They both read 9:22 a.m. It was then she noticed the buzzing noise. It was a hum of sorts that she couldn't place.

She got out of bed and went to her window to see why it was so dark. The entire window, or what was on the other side of the curtain, was moving. She couldn't make sense of what she was seeing, and confusion gave way to trepidation as she felt something other than soft carpet under feet. It made crunching noises each time she took a step.

She was afraid to pull the curtains back, and afraid of what she might see behind them. Bracing herself for what, she didn't know ... to scream, run, sit down and cry ... she called Coraline over to her side. Hesitantly the dog came to her, whining and sniffing the air, elevating Hazel's fear. If the dog sensed danger, something was wrong.

With one hand on Coraline and clenching her eyes tightly closed, too afraid to take in what was lurking behind the curtain all at once, she grasped the curtain and yanked it back. Nothing jumped out at her, but as she opened her eyes something touched her face. The sight stole her breath and stopped the cry building in her chest. On the outside of the window was what she could only comprehend as a swarm of bugs. One had landed on her face, and she brushed it away. Insects covered every inch of the window, blocking the light from outside. The bugs had breached the sill, and a line of insects were crawling down the wall. Others were taking flight, while some crawled across the floor. She turned to see where they were going. The mural was in motion; the entire wall was undulating and buzzing.

She rushed to her light switch as several of the bugs landed in her hair. She swatted at them madly. When the chandelier illuminated the room, she was horrified by what she saw—the bugs had obliterated the mural, covering the entire wall. Some had landed in her bed while others lay lifeless on the floor. Coraline was barking furiously and lunging at the wall.

She stared as the swarm moved frantically in a dizzying dance. She was too mesmerized to move. They were thousands and thousands of ladybugs. More bugs landed in her hair, breaking her from her frozen stare. She called Coraline away from the wall and backed out of the room, grabbing the dog by her collar. Every time she set her foot down, she could hear the crunching sound of dozens of bugs being crushed under feet. She slammed the door behind her and ran, not sure where she was going. As she raced down the stairs, she yelled, "Mom!"

Mom exited the living room with a worried expression on her face. Hazel, in her panicked state, collided with her as she came around the corner. Unable to complete a coherent sentence, Hazel grabbed Mom's wrist and said, "Come!" She half-dragged, half-led Mom back upstairs. As they approached the bedroom door, Hazel could hear the droning of the bug's wings beyond the door and was afraid to open it. She paused with her hand on the knob, and saw several of the ladybugs had escaped her room and were crawling on the carpet just beyond the threshold.

"What's going on, Hazel?" Mom asked impatiently.

Hazel couldn't answer that question, so she threw the door open. She was sure that more bugs had entered her room just in the few minutes she had been gone. A few of them made a break for the door. Mom stood with her mouth agape, speechless. Hazel slammed the door before more bugs could escape.

"What ... What's happening in there?" Mom uttered, finally finding words. Hazel did not have answers. Coraline was clawing at the door. "I'm going to get Dad."

Hazel followed, not wanting to stay alone so close to the horde of the gentle insects.

The two went to Dad's office and entered without knocking. Before he could get upset about the intrusion, he noticed his wife's pale face as she said, "Come quick! There are bugs all over Hazel's room!"

As the three ascended the stairs, Dad couldn't help but question the belief that bugs were an emergency that warranted interrupting his workday.

"Sorry ladies, I know bugs might freak you out, but maybe you could've asked Holden to help you. I'm sure he could dig up a can of bug spray and take care of the problem."

"You have to see for yourself, Dad. Bug spray isn't going to fix this," Hazel said, unable to prepare Dad for what he was about to see.

Dad didn't hear the buzzing sound and reached for the door, opening it before Hazel or Mom could stop him. Their numbers had grown, all the bugs in flight or crawling to the mural. Some flew off course and headed toward Dad as he leaned inside the room to get a better look. He swatted the bugs away before they could land, closed the door, and stood silent, unsure of what to do or say next.

"Maybe we should call Dave," he finally said, already dialing the number for Critter Getters as he descended the stairs.

Critter Getter Dave arrived within a couple of hours, and Hazel couldn't help but wonder what her room looked like by that time. She envisioned the entire room with every inch taken over by the bugs. Dave started his probe outside at the back of the house, where Hazel's bedroom window was. The swarm had begun to dissipate, taking flight to other areas around the yard and woods.

After looking things over in Hazel's room, he told Mom and Dad, through a mask, "There is a small gap between the frame and the wall. That's their entry point. I don't have an answer yet as to why they were drawn to that spot. There's no food source in the bedroom, so it really doesn't make much sense yet. But I sealed the crack so no more can get in. I'm gonna get my ladder and take a look. I'll also look at the tree outside the window and see if it holds any clues."

After checking a few more things, Dave descended the ladder and joined the anxious family on the back lawn. "Well, folks, what you have here is called a loveliness—it's the official term for a large gathering of ladybugs. I've honestly never seen anything like it in all my years. It isn't uncommon to have a swarm of flying ants or termites inside the house. I see that stuff all the time, but this is a first for me!"

Mom cringed at the thought of termites. Dad said, "Well, I guess ladybugs are better than termites."

"Yep, you'd be right about that. Sometimes, after an unseasonable cold snap, folks will see clusters of ladybugs inside. They move toward warmth. Cooler temperatures sure sound nice right now," Dave said, wiping the sweat out of his eyes. "But given the heat, it doesn't make sense for them to have swarmed the house. Now that they can no longer get inside, I can start the removal. With termites and ants, people don't care much about being humane. They just want the things gone, so we fumigate and vacuum up their carcasses."

"You're going to kill them?" said Hazel.

"Well, that was my next question. The way I see it, there are a few ways to go about removing the buggers. I can open the window and use some nets to remove as many as I can and just toss them out. Some are bound to escape, but I'll do my best. Hate to say it, but you'll likely be finding the darn things for some time to come, either alive or dead."

"Stands to reason," said Dad.

"So, if you don't know why they came into the house, there is no guarantee they won't come back? There's nothing you can do, like use a spray or a bomb? Anything?" Mom inquired, still unsure about entire situation.

"Can't rightly say why they showed up. Typically, they would only show up en masse to feed, usually on aphids, which I didn't see signs of in the tree. Pretty sure you haven't got a roomful of aphids now, do you, kid?" Dave directed his inquiry to Hazel. She was almost sure he was joking.

He laughed. "Of course you don't! Anyway, I wouldn't recommend exterminating the ladybugs. Most people like having them around. They are good for gardens and keep the bad guys of the insect world away. No ma'am, I don't think spraying would be right. I'll clear out what I can and take a look around all the other windows. With a house this big, it might take a while," he said, delivering his message in a probing manner, as if preparing Dad for the bill.

"Um, yeah, Dave. Please, if you've got the time, we would appreciate it if you could take a look and seal up anything you find that needs sealing. I certainly don't want another loveliness of ladybugs or something worse invading the house," Dad said.

"Will do, Mr. Weizak," Dave said. Turning his attention to Mom, "Don't you worry, Mrs. Weizak. I'll get things fixed up and I wouldn't expect it to happen again. One of those flukes of nature, I reckon. I have to say, this is going in the record books for the most interesting call of the year!"

The family retreated to the kitchen while Dave completed his inspection and removal. "Well, this is definitely another head-scratcher," Dad said when they had all taken a seat.

"This house, I just ..." Mom chimed in, shaking her head in disbelief.

Holden couldn't resist pushing Mom's buttons. "What if it had been roaches instead of ladybugs?"

Mom gave him "the look." Hazel, who hadn't thought of anything worse than ladybugs, was grateful it had been a cute bug. She would be a million times more freaked out if it had been some gross insect. But Holden had a lot of nerve joking about it when his room was bug free.

"I've got to get back to work," said Dad. "I think you should all stay downstairs until Dave is done."

Holden and Hazel hung out in the family room while Mom busied herself in the kitchen.

The summer sun was sinking low in the sky by the time Dave finished the job. They joined him outside.

"Well," he said, "I have to say I'm impressed with myself. I think I got almost every last one of the things. The little 'ladies' were cooperative."

He could see the relief on their faces, even hidden behind masks.

"Thank you so much, Dave!" Mom gushed.

"I'd recommend giving the bedding a good washing with hot water. You might be finding them inside your shoes and such. But, hey, if you had to have an infestation, I can't think of anything lovelier than ladybugs."

Holden provided a rim shot. "Ba dum tssh!"

Hazel rolled her eyes, and no one else was ready to laugh about the day's events.

That night while eating a late dinner, Dad began his inquiry into the midnight Alexa reminder. The incident was nearly forgotten by the twins, with the appearance of the ladybugs having taken center stage. Holden insisted he had nothing to do with setting the reminder, as did Hazel.

Holden was quick to point out, "Mom's phone is essentially the gatekeeper for the app. If her phone wasn't used to set the reminder, that means someone had to go to each room and tell every device individually, and turn the volume up on all of them too. Sorry, my time is far too valuable to waste on some lame prank. Besides, there's no way I'm doing something so pointless to mess with my sleep."

Mom scrolled through the Alexa app on her phone, searching the Activity tab. There it was—the device had been told to remind them to check the pool, and the scheduled alert was for 12:00 a.m. There was no way to tell who Alexa had received the directive from.

Holden walked over to the Echo Show that sat on the kitchen counter. He hit the volume button and pointed out,

"The volume is set to fifty percent. It sounded like Alexa was yelling through the house last night."

"Maybe we've been hacked," Mom wondered. She had heard stories of people's home security systems and smart devices falling victim to hackers in ways that seemed childish or sometimes perverse. She started searching for information on her phone about people hacking home automation technology.

"Someone had to have a lot of time on their hands to decide to hack into the Weizaks' Alexa to set reminders telling them to check the pool," noted Dad.

Mom looked up from her research and said, "Well, did you check the pool?" Dad was taken aback by the question.

Mom hadn't meant the question to sound critical, just inquisitive.

Dad chuckled. "Well," he admitted. "I usually take a look at it every day, but between work and the ladybugs, I didn't even think of checking the pool today. I'll be sure to take a look at it tomorrow." They cleaned up their dinner mess and went into the living room. They searched Amazon Prime and agreed on an action flick to watch in hopes of taking their minds off the turbulent events that were now taking place inside the house as well as all over the world.

Mom double-checked the Alexa app before she went to bed, to make sure no reminder had been set that would awaken them in the middle of the night. This was after the nightly running of the stairs, which at this point barely fazed any of them. None of them had noticed that the runner now stopped short outside Hazel's room, but Dad patted himself on the back for fixing the issue with the garage door camera.

After checking with Holden, Mom popped into Hazel's room and asked her devices if there were any reminders set, to which Alexa replied, "You have no reminders." She got the same response in the home gym. Feeling confident that their sleep would not be interrupted that night, she wished the twins good night and reminded them to not stay up too late.

Staying up too late wasn't a possibility for Hazel. She had fought to stay awake during the day, since her sleep was invaded more and more by the baffling nightmare. She found herself nodding off several times during the day while watching TikTok videos or trying to read, and she had even fallen asleep during the movie.

After putting fresh bedding on her bed, she made a sweep of the area, clearing out surprisingly few lady bugs. She recounted the painted ladybugs on the mural and could have sworn she had counted twelve ladybugs the day she had decided not to paint over it. Today she counted twenty-six. She also noted that the brook seemed to be changing colors, taking on an eerie reddish tint. It must be a trick of the lighting, she told herself.

"Alexa, play forty-five minutes of Sleep Sounds."

Alexa responded, "Sleep Sounds for forty-five minutes, starting now." But Alexa didn't play Sleep Sounds. She played a song by Tears for Fears. Hazel recognized it immediately—it was "Mad World."

"Alexa, stop," she said and waited a few seconds before trying again. "Alexa, play Sleep Sounds." Once again, Alexa agreed to play the requested playlist, but when the audio started it was yet another Tears for Fears song, this time "Memories Fade."

Hazel was getting annoyed. It was as if the AI—artificial yes, intelligence ... that was kind of a stretch—was losing her "mind."

"Alexa, stop!" Hazel exclaimed. The music abruptly ceased as requested. Hazel considered asking for Sleep Sounds again but was too tired and irritated to argue with the device. She threw the blankets over here head, and as she nodded off hoped that she would sleep peacefully, free of confusing and frightening nightmares.

Less than two hours later her sleep was disturbed again by Alexa's voice, this time loudly imploring, "I'm reminding you, please check the pool." Hazel bolted up from bed and shouted for Alexa to stop before she could finish repeating the phrase a second time. She could hear the phrase as it resonated on the other devices throughout the house.

Coraline was at the door again, barking incessantly, and she could hear Phineas in her parents' room doing the same. She got up and was making her way across the room when her foot became entangled in something on the floor. Unable to stop her momentum, she went down. She wasn't hurt by the fall, but when she realized what she had tripped on, she couldn't believe what she was seeing. Her bedroom floor was covered in clothes —specifically her swimsuits and cover-ups. The drawer where she kept her swim gear was standing open, empty.

Coraline was sniffing the suits, fur on end, growling. Hazel got to her feet and made a dash to the door. Outside, she found her mom standing in front of the workout room, yelling for Alexa to stop. Dad was running down the stairs to the silence the Show and the Dot on the lower level. Holden must have been in a deep sleep because he was just then telling his Dot to stop.

As Dad came back upstairs he said, "I unplugged the devices downstairs; you might want to do the same up here." He was obviously angered by being startled awake for a second night.

Holden tried to lighten the mood. "At least she said please this time." No one laughed.

"Everyone go back to bed," said Mom.

Hazel went back to her room and gathered up the suits, stuffing them back into the drawer. All the while, she wondered who had come into her bedroom and made the mess without waking her. She decided to sleep with the door open and her light on, resisting the urge go to her parents' room and ask to sleep with them. She hadn't wanted to do that since she was a young child and she and Holden got their own bedrooms, but she was becoming very unnerved by the things that were happening in the house.

She was afraid of what she might see when she closed her eyes. She was afraid of the nightmares, and what she might wake up to in the morning. Holden would never let her hear the end of it if she took her pillow and tried to sleep in her parents' room. It wasn't as if she would crawl in between the two of them like she did when she was a kid; that would just be weird. They had a couch in their room, a comfortable couch. She lay in bed considering the idea and playing out how her parents might react to the request. In the end, she decided to suck it up and deal with it. Having the door open and light on might help. Maybe.

Sleep eluded her for a long while, despite her exhaustion. She wasn't sure how long she had been asleep when the nightmare began. She was running through puddles in a thunderstorm. In the dream she was afraid—terrified, actually. She stopped at the edge of a cliff or ledge of some sort. Lightning lit up the sky and thunder crashed loudly, causing her to jump. She turned and in the burst of light saw what she thought was the figure of a man just at the edge of a tree line. She began falling, and then there was water. The water was red, and she was unable to reach the surface ...

She woke, gasping, her face wet with tears. She sat up in bed, trying to shake the terrifying images and emotions the nightmare always brought. There in the doorway of her bedroom stood a figure. She froze. The person had been watching her sleep but disappeared very quickly; not turning to walk away, simply vanishing. She recognized the person, even though it was someone she had never met before. She only caught a glimpse of the girl but for a moment, she knew she had seen Laura Combs.

There was no way she could spend the rest of the night in this room. She grabbed her pillow and comforter and jumped out of bed. Coraline woke and dutifully followed in her footsteps, both of them stepping on her swimsuits that were again strewn about the floor. She hesitated at her doorway, afraid to breach the space where she had just witnessed the ... Apparition? Ghost? Closing her eyes tightly and grasping Coraline's collar with her free hand, she bolted across the threshold.

She didn't know what she had expected, maybe a bone-chilling cold spot? She felt nothing out of the ordinary but could smell the faint smell of rain. Relieved to be in the hall, she sprinted to her parents' bedroom. She knocked quietly on their door, as to not wake Holden up. She didn't wait for a reply before opening the door and whispering, "Mom, I need to sleep in your room tonight."

From his spot at the end of the bed, Phineas looked up disinterestedly.

Mom lifted her head and groggily asked, "Are you okay, Haze? Is everything all right?"

Hazel whispered, "Yeah, I'm fine, just a little freaked out."

"Okay," she said. "Why don't you take the couch?" Within minutes Hazel could hear Mom's rhythmic breaths, signaling she had quickly fallen back asleep.

Getting herself situated, she felt foolish. Coraline whined from the floor. Scooting back, she made room for the dog and quietly patted the couch. There was barely enough space for her, much less the dog, but she couldn't think of a better alternative. Her own bedroom was a hard pass for the night.

Hazel began to settle in. The sounds of Dad's snoring and

Mom's soft breathing relaxed her and calmed her heart rate. She was comforted by the dog's weight and warmth. She stared at the darkness, reliving scenes of the nightmare in a failed attempt to quiet the memory of the person standing in her door, the swimsuits thrown about her room. To ease her frightened mind, she forced herself to believe that she hadn't indeed seen the ghost of Laura Combs. Instead, a tiny rational voice told her it was her imagination; that lack of sleep and the stress of the move, the pandemic, the weirdness of it all, had compelled her to conjure the girl. It was the only explanation she could accept that allowed her to not freak out completely. Without that acceptance, she would flip out and beg her parents to call a psychic, a priest, sell the house, something, anything.

She did her best to hush the voices that told her she hadn't dreamed that Laura Combs was watching her. That this time Laura didn't need an app to make herself known. Try as she might to convince herself an over-stressed mind dreamed up the girl, what haunted her the most about the figure of Laura Combs was that she'd seen the girl as she appeared in the original missing poster. It hadn't been the age-progressed image, the Laura Combs who looked so much like her mother, not the middle-aged Laura Combs. She had seen the thirteen-year-old Laura Combs.

Mom and Dad were going about their morning routine in an exaggerated tiptoeing fashion as to not wake her. Levels of embarrassment overshadowed those of confusion as Hazel fully visualized the scene. She felt foolish for running to her parents' room in the middle of the night like a child scared by a bad dream. But it wasn't just a bad dream, and seeking security on their couch wasn't the worst part of the awkward situation.

She sat up to let them know they didn't need to keep quiet any longer and hoped they wouldn't press for an explanation. She was already trying to formulate her escape plan in hopes that Holden wouldn't see her exiting their room, pillow and blanket in hand.

"Good morning, sunshine!" Dad cheerfully exclaimed. He was always abundantly peppy on Friday mornings. "Mom said you had a rough night. Well, rougher than the rest of us. Seems Alexa or whatever doesn't want us to get a good night's sleep these days. Anywho, you doing okay now?"

Hazel paused, considering whether she should tell her parents about the mess in her room and what she saw in her doorway. Would they believe her? Would they laugh? She decided to hold off. She still hadn't really processed it herself.

"Um, yeah, Dad, I'm okay. Sorry to crash the party."

"No problem, kid. Hope my snoring didn't keep you up. Looks like this rain will let up in time for the Fourth. We ought to do it up right tomorrow. Food, pool, music, fireworks. Can't wait!"

Hazel was making her way toward the door, hoping Holden wasn't up yet. "Sounds great, Dad. Looking forward to it. Thanks for the crash pad." She felt immediate relief when she saw Holden's door closed and the hallway quiet.

She paused at the door to her room, hand hovering above the doorknob, reluctant to open it for fear of what she might see. She closed her eyes, pushed the door open and counted to three before opening her eyes. As expected, all was not in its place. This time, the tapestries she had used to cover the walls were torn down and now lay in puddles on the floor among the swim wear. *HELP LAURA COMBS* practically screamed from the walls, written in an angry red instead of the pasty color from before.

Hot tears spilled onto her face, and she wished she would have picked a paint color already. Normally she would have blamed Holden. Nothing was normal these days, and she knew her brother wouldn't bother with making messes in her room, and he would never paint over the message in this angry red. Mom and Dad would come up with some lame explanation. She was alone on this one. She quickly rehung the tapestries, blocking out the urgent message for now.

She was now resolute that a paint color be selected, so she opened her MacBook to begin her search. She was face-to-face with Laura again. This time it was a two-dimensional image staring back at her. It was the original missing poster in a browser window she had left open.

She slammed the notebook closed as visions of the girl standing outside her bedroom flooded her mind. Wishing for nothing more than to escape all the madness surrounding Laura Combs, she decided to continue her search downstairs, away from the bed where nightmares plagued her sleep, the wall that pleaded with her for help, the window and its memory of the ladybug kaleidoscope, and the doorway where Laura Combs herself stood the night before.

The family spent the day inside, doing chores. Holden wasn't pleased with the intrusion on his gaming time, but Hazel welcomed the distraction. When the chores were done, Mom helped Hazel decide on a paint color and placed the order. Hazel saw the expected delivery date and stopped herself from begging Mom to pay for expedited shipping. After spending a day going about normal daily tasks, Hazel was convinced that telling her parents about the vision of Laura Combs, and the added urgency to the message on her wall, might end up with her being forced into a virtual session with a psychologist. Then again, she wondered if that might be exactly what she needed.

That night all the Alexa devices were unplugged. The family was in the living room watching a movie when the nightly stair run occurred. No one bothered to pause and take notice, and no one mentioned the abrupt stop midway down the hall. Even the dogs barely gave a chuff.

As they headed upstairs Hazel held her breath, fearing Mom or Dad might ask if she was planning on camping out on their couch again. The subject had not come up all day, and she was certain if she could just make it past this point Holden would never know.

Holden, being deprived of gaming the entire day, couldn't wait to get back to his computer. He rushed past them. "Good night, parental units, fair twin, sweet dreams to you all!" And he disappeared into his bedroom.

Hazel's relief was quickly clouded by the realization that her only alternatives were to sleep alone in her room or ask her parents for a couch pass again. Deciding she didn't want to face the embarrassment, she hugged her parents and said, "Good night!" before heading to her bathroom to get ready for bed. She stood in the darkened doorway of her bedroom, dreading what she might find when she turned on the light. She flipped the switch and the blood-red words leaped from the walls in a blinding pulse. The tapestries had been removed again.

"Stop, please. I don't know how to help you. I'm sorry," she whispered to the empty room as she gathered the clothing that had been thrown about the room. She hurriedly flipped on her bedside lamp and turned the overhead light off. Softer light might soften the effect. She crumpled to the floor with a bundle of clothes in her hands and tears streaming down her face. The exhaustion and fear overwhelmed her and she felt helpless. Resigning herself to cover the words again, she stood on shaky feet and saw the words begin to lose color. Each letter slowly fading to pink before returning to their original, subdued hue. Even though this was more alarming than the first change, when the words went from a pale whisper to a red siren, and it was happening right before her eyes, she was more grateful for the change than scared by it and quietly said, "'Thank you."

Shaken and restless, she hoped a long FaceTime sesh with Miren might help. But the edginess did not subside as she filled her friend in on all the unusual things that had been taking place, including the nightmares and the rude awakenings in the night. Hesitantly, she told Miren about seeing Laura Combs in her room.

"Whoa, Haze, have you checked your temperature lately? I'm not completely sure, but I think hallucinations might be a symptom of the virus," Miren joked.

"Mir, seriously, I don't know what to do. And to make matters worse, we are all just stuck here. It's not like you can head out for a day of shopping to take your mind off any of it." Her voice betrayed the tears she tried to hide. The claustrophobic nature of the situation made the whole thing a million times more dismal.

"I'm sorry. I hear you. My mom won't let me go anywhere. I am so over skateboarding up and down my own street. At least you have a pool. Everything is closed here, including the parks. But, yeah, I don't have a ghost, my cat didn't die, and my Alexa isn't losing her mind. So, okay, you win. By a landslide." Miren could always make Hazel laugh, which was what she needed right now, and she couldn't help but laugh at Miren's take on her completely insane situation.

"I don't know what to tell you, sorry," continued her friend. "Hold a séance, burn some sage?"

Hazel laughed again. "Very valuable suggestions."

"Facts!" replied Miren.

Both girls were still laughing when the tablet screen began to glitch and Miren's face became a digitized Picasso rendering —an all-too-familiar sight in the days of constant Zoom meetings and Google Hangouts. Before Hazel gave up on their connection, the image became crisp again, only this time it wasn't Miren's face framed by the usual backdrop of her eclectic bedroom. The image that came forth was Laura Comb's face, peering at her from a murky blackness.

Hazel couldn't believe what she was seeing, but she couldn't look away. She jumped with shock, shoving the notebook away when what she thought was a static image lurched to life in a terrifying twitch and began to speak.

"Help me."

Tears ran down Hazel's cheeks, and a feeling of complete helplessness crashed upon her as the Macbook landed on its side and the girl continued to speak.

"Help me."

She grabbed the device and slammed it shut. With trembling hands, she shoved it under her bed, wanting to distance herself from it.

Anger rose inside her. She had been feeling so good for the first time in forever. The long-overdue conversation with Miren had released much of the tension that had become her normal state. Seeing her best friend, laughing with her, had made her feel so much better, lessening the feeling of utter isolation. Of course nothing was solved. Miren couldn't offer her any sound advice, but getting some of it off her chest and sharing it with someone outside of the house had helped. To have it interrupted in such a manner brought back the feeling of helplessness. She didn't understand why she was being harassed like this. It really was harassment; she couldn't think of another word to describe the events and was angered by the relentless nature of the torment.

She had hoped all day for a good night's rest, and now it came due to sheer exhaustion as she lay in bed crying. At first, it was a deep sleep, so peaceful that she didn't hear the odd chime from her phone about thirty minutes after she crashed out.

The nightmare didn't stay away for long. The storm, the running, confusing imagery in the trees alight by lightning flashes, falling, being under water, red water, desperation, fear. She woke, thrashing and crying, as if she were trying to save herself from imminent peril. She reached for her phone to check the time. In her notification center was one icon she didn't often see, but she recognized. She clicked on the icon and was chilled by what she saw. She had missed the notification at midnight reminding her to check the pool. She dropped her phone and saw the open drawer and swimsuits lying about her floor. She grabbed her pillow and threw it over her head. Then she pulled her comforter on top of that and drew Coraline close. She refused to open her eyes, refused to acknowledge anything until the sun came up.

TWENTY

Her hair clung to her face in a sweaty mess when she woke buried under a pile of pillows and blankets. Hot, grumpy, and far from well rested, she threw back the covers and lay in bed for some time contemplating her situation.

Something had to give soon. She couldn't go on sleeping so poorly and living in fear of what she might see in her bedroom when she woke. There was no way Holden would agree to swapping rooms with her. Maybe her parents would let her move into the workout room and relocate the fitness equipment into this room. It would be weird having her own washer and dryer, and Holden might complain about her getting an en suite bathroom. But the workout room was way smaller and again, having laundry machines in your room was pretty weird. Plus, there was no guarantee a move would make it all go away.

Begrudgingly, she got out of bed and headed down to let Coraline out. She didn't bother picking up the tangle of swimsuits that lay on her floor.

Mom and Dad were in the kitchen. Dad was already sporting his *License to Grill* apron and was prepping his "world-famous" ribs. Mom was busily making her "world-famous" potato salad. The people who had deemed these recipes world-famous remained a mystery to Hazel.

"Happy Fourth, Haze! How'd you sleep?" asked Mom.

"Better than some nights," she replied in a tone that was part sarcasm, part *I'm still half asleep.*

Dad chimed in, "I bet a day of soaking in some rays will make you feel right as rain. I'm making my world-famous ribs!"

Hazel trudged past them, wondering if Dad realized what he'd said or if he intended the oxymoron to be a joke. She decided not to mention anything about the FaceTime crasher, swimsuit drawer raider, nor the middle of the night pool reminder on her phone, but did wonder if she was the only one who had gotten the mysterious reminder. She went upstairs to change, picking a swimsuit from the pile on her floor. Outside her window she heard Mom hollering at Dad. She opened her curtains and found dozens of ladybug carcasses on the window ledge. Her parents were prepping the pool for the festivities, and she gave herself a little pep talk in an attempt to brush off her foul mood. She could see her parents were going to great lengths to make the best of their quarantine Independence Day celebration.

Mom was already in the pool and Dad was at the grill when she joined them outside. The backyard looked as if guests were expected. The over-the-top decorations were too much for just the four of them. A new umbrella spanned the table that was filled with snacks and drinks. A celebratory playlist provided the perfect ambiance for the festive scene. New floats bobbed in the crystal pool and sunlight played on the water.

Even Phineas had a new inflatable. The dog looked ridiculous lounging on the float that was adorned with dog bones and collars, but Mom thought it was the most adorable thing ever as she guided him around the water, gushing about how cute he was.

As Hazel opened the safety gate, Coraline rushed past her, spying her water toy afloat near Phin's tiny boat. The dog galloped full speed and catapulted from the edge of the pool, knocking Phineas into the water; the little dog sank some distance before bobbing to the surface. The commotion knocked Mom's sunhat off her head, but she ignored it in her pursuit of saving her precious Phineas as he swam for the safety of the stairs.

Coraline paid no heed to the chaos she had caused as she came up from beneath the waves, toy in mouth, and paddled to the pool's edge. Mom made it to the stairs just in time for both dogs to climb out of the water and shake themselves off, showering her with wet dog droplets. Her sun hat drifting among the new floats punctuated the lunacy of the scene.

Dad was unaware of the calamity behind him as he carefully monitored the grill. Hazel wished she'd had her phone out to record the whole thing.

Holden walked out to find Hazel standing alone on the patio, cracking up.

"What'd I miss?" he said as the two descended the stairs.

"You wouldn't believe me if I told you."

They feasted on ribs, corn on the cob, potato salad, and soda under the shade of the umbrella. Dad and Holden discussed the best spot to shoot off the fireworks left over from last year's normal celebration. After overeating, Mom and Dad cleaned up while Holden and Hazel did their best to wear Coraline out. They tossed her toy into the water over and over as the dog splashed in, dove deep, and retrieved the toy to drop it at their feet. It never got old, at least not to the dog.

Coraline did tire eventually and lay on the cool deck, drying in the sun as she dozed off. Phineas performed a thorough sweep under the table, gobbling up crumbs, then picked a spot to lie in the sun.

Holden grabbed the water football, took position at the not-so-deep, deep end, and tossed the ball to Hazel who stood in the shallow end. Mom and Dad got into the pool, awkwardly maneuvering themselves onto a new two-person float.

"What do you say, family? Isn't this turning out to be a great day?" Dad said, after finally getting himself into what he hoped was a stable position.

"Definitely," Mom chimed in. "Perfect weather, awesome food, good tunes... We are all together, safe and healthy. We couldn't ask for more!"

Hazel agreed, and she was feeling better than she had in days but hoped Holden would tire of tossing the football so she could take a nap on a float.

Even Holden forgot, for the time being, about what he might be missing online.

"Stellar day, Boomers!" he said, lifting the football overhead. Before he could release the ball, he felt a shift in the floor of the pool. His mind struggled to grasp what was happening as his foot sank deeper into the floor of the pool, dragging him beneath the waters' surface.

The holiday playlist stopped abruptly and was replaced by "Mad World" as Hazel saw a crack opening on the floor of the pool. A deep crevice slowly crawled across the bottom of the pool, moving toward her. The water sloshed wildly, spilling over the sides. Mom and Dad were knocked off their float.

Hazel's first thought was earthquake. Earthquakes weren't unheard-of in Oklahoma, and the family had been through a couple. Before these thoughts could culminate cohesively in her mind, something vile began to spill up from the fractured floor, permeating the pool as the crack grew wider, turning the water red.

"Get out of the pool!" she screamed, clambering for the stairs. "Get out of the water, now!"

Holden had already seen what Hazel had and was attempting to free himself from the undertow and lift himself out of the pool. The red substance bubbled up from the crack as blood might, from a deep wound. He struggled to escape, not wanting the red water to touch him, but was sucked back down into the growing chasm. He reached the surface in full-on panic and screamed for help. He had never been so scared.

Dad took action, his mind in fight mode as a rush of adrenaline gave him the strength to push Mom to the edge and boost her up out of the water. He lifted himself out next and ran to Holden, grabbing his hands and hoisting his son up.

The water continued to splash from side to side in ever mounting waves and the red anomaly blotted out the crystal blue water, leaving the pool looking like a literal blood bath. Both dogs barked feverishly at the edge of the deck, and the family grabbed onto one another, watching the ordeal in shock. The splashing subsided and after a few minutes the water was calm, though still red. The crack extended from one end to the other, just beyond each edge, at least eight inches wide. It looked as if the entire pool would collapse inward and disappear into the earth.

Dad looked up at the house. There was no apparent damage to indicate an earthquake of a magnitude that would cause this kind of damage.

"Stay here," he told the three as he cautiously approached the crack. Dozens of scorpions and centipedes writhed to escape the grip of twisted roots in the fissure that extended beyond the water's edge. "Everyone inside!" he yelled.

Once inside, Mom fussed over Holden first, grabbing a wad of paper towels, wiping his face and scrubbing his hair, the towel turning crimson as she did.

"Are you all right? Were you hurt?" Being assured by the twins that they had not been injured, she began searching the walls and ceiling, checking for signs that an earthquake had been the cause. But nothing was disturbed. A quick glance at social media proved that a tremor had not been felt by the masses. "What was that?" She now looked to Dad for answers.

He had none. "I have no idea," was all he had to offer.

With a shaky voice, Mom suggested, "We should all take showers, wash off whatever that might have been. What if it is some kind of chemical! Go! Go, take a shower. Now!"

TWENTY-ONE

The search for a pool company that could address the abomination was slowed by the holiday weekend, but Dad found one in Oklahoma City. There was no time for vetting the best, so he took the first available. None of them wanted to look in the backyard to see what was happening with the pool.

Holden and Hazel took Phineas and Coraline out the front door, avoiding the backyard altogether. Mom closed all the curtains and blinds. She could block out the view, but not the memory of what had happened.

By the time Bryce Gleason with Sunscapes, Inc. showed up on Monday morning, the pool water level had dropped by almost a foot but the unsettling cerise hue remained. Bryce let out an ear-splitting whistle just as Dad opened the back door to meet Mr. Gleason outside. The man's reaction sent the dogs into a barking frenzy that further unraveled Mom's frayed nerves. Hazel shushed the dogs and then separated the blinds to watch as Dad showed Mr. Gleason the damage.

The men spent an hour looking at the pool from seemingly every angle. They crouched down, maintaining distance from each other, while Mr. Gleason pointed to various things related to the pool and land. Dad nodded, looking dispirited even with half his face hidden behind a mask. When they finished their conversation, each man put their hands out in the long familiar and customary manner of shaking on it, but caught themselves before completing the act. Instead, they shared an awkward elbow bump, and Mr. Gleason walked back to his car and drove away.

Dad stood in the middle of the yard looking from the quote Mr. Gleason had provided to the pool, shaking his head in disbelief. Reentering the house, he handed the paper to Mom. "It's about as bad as we thought."

Mom looked over the estimate. She had nothing to say.

"I had him go ahead and quote a diving pool. We might as well spring for it now since the whole thing has to be dug up anyway. Oh, and I promised you all a diving pool. I just didn't expect to get it so soon and under such unusual circumstances. He said they could have someone here tomorrow to start draining it, so work can start later this week."

"Should we get a second quote? Have someone else take a look?" Mom asked without looking up from the paperwork.

"We probably should. This will eat up our remodeling budget," agreed Dad. "But honestly, I just want to get it started, so we can get it over with. I don't want any more delays. I'm already tired of looking at the eyesore."

Handing the estimate back, Mom agreed. "You're right. I'd rather not waste any time. I can't stand looking at that, whatever that is. Let's get started. And yes, let's make it a diving pool."

The next day James Wheeler showed up to drain the pool. Mr. Wheeler did contract work for Sunscapes and owned a pool cleaning service in town, so he had the equipment necessary to start the process. He provided his own reluctant explanation.

"Stillwater is known for its red dirt and that crack goes pretty deep," he said. "I'm guessing the dirt is giving the water its bloody appearance."

This explanation came as a great relief to the family. It was far better than some toxic spill or biological material, really any of the frightful causes that had been playing out in their minds.

Mr. Wheeler started the pump. "I'll be back in a few hours to check on it," he said as he got in his truck.

Hazel stood at the window and watched as the pool slowly emptied, reliving the terrible events. Holden had scarcely left his room since retreating there after his shower the day before.

There had been no further reminders from Alexa to check the pool. Had the AI somehow sensed the impending disaster that awaited them while swimming? That was an unsettling notion. A psychic Alexa—crazy, yes, but crazier things had happened so far that year. Hazel wondered if the unknown entity was happy now. The pool had been checked after all. Shrugging her shoulders to no one but her own scattered thoughts, she turned her back on the receding red waters of the pool and retreated to her room. Miren was never going to believe this latest occurrence. She didn't have the courage to attempt to FaceTime her best friend, so she just made a phone call.

By the end of the day the pool was empty, and a few inches of thick, red mud clung to the large crack. Mr. Wheeler set up some orange cones and caution tape, as if anyone would see the empty shell as inviting.

TWENTY-TWO

A day later, heavy machinery arrived to break up the cracked cement so a deeper hole could be dug to the depth needed for a diving pool. Unfortunately, there would be no more swimming until next summer, but the season would be winding down soon anyway. The family continued to avoid the backyard. No longer repulsed by the red water, but repelled on a more visceral level, something they sensed warned them to steer clear.

Mr. Wheeler, having been in the town and the business for many years, called in favors and was able to obtain an "emergency" permit to expedite the process.

The concrete was quickly broken up and hauled away, but a few stormy days delayed digging.

The family had taken to eating in the formal dining room, distancing themselves from the slow progress and to avoid being reminded of their last day in the pool. But the distance wasn't far enough to block out the noise as the rain delay ended and work began.

They sat eating a lunch of leftovers as a familiar brown

truck stopped in front of their house. The driver placed a package on their doorstep with practiced speed. Without speaking, Mom grabbed sanitizing wipes and spray and retrieved the package before the driver had made his way back onto Sheffield Court.

"It's Bailey's memorial stone," she said sadly, as she went about killing off any germs. "I can't wait to see it, but it will have to sit here for twenty minutes before we can open it." The reminder wasn't necessary, since Mom's sanitizing system was now just part of their own new norm. The trio heard the foot pedal of the trashcan and water running as Mom washed her hands far longer than the recommended twenty seconds. She returned to the entryway, placing her cleaning materials back in the closet.

As she joined the group at the table to finish her lunch, she asked, "Has anyone had any weird experiences lately?"

Hazel spoke first. "Not really. Things have quieted down, even the running sound on the stairs." She had still told no one besides Miren of her sighting of Laura Combs, nor of all the other troubling incidents she had experienced.

Holden agreed. "You're right. Alexa hasn't reminded me of anything I didn't need to be reminded of. She's only played the music I've asked her to play, and I haven't seen any ghostly specters in the hallway lately. Nice catch, Mom."

This was the first time Holden had given any hint he had issues with Alexa's music options and that he may have also seen Laura Combs. Well, he didn't say it had been Laura Combs, but rather a "ghostly specter" in the hallway. She needed to know more. Maybe when they were alone, she would have a better chance to pry some details out of him.

"Well, I guess that's one thing to be thankful for," Dad said, getting up with his empty plate. "Gotta get back to the rat race.

Bring the memorial stone in and show me if you don't mind. Once it isn't a biohazard, that is."

Mom wasn't fazed by their jabs about her extreme germ avoidance measures. "Sure thing, hon. Have a good afternoon. I'll take that for you," she said, taking his plate and giving him a peck on the cheek. She left the twins in the dining room to busy herself in the kitchen.

Hazel pushed her plate back and turned to Holden. "Did you actually see something in the hallway?"

Holden was still chewing his food but Hazel detected a brief pause, and she could see the question had thrown him off as he realized he had let more slip than he had intended. Finally, he spoke. "I'm really not up to such a controversial topic. Maybe we could have a lively discussion about say, politics or religion."

"I'm serious. I won't think you are crazy, because I saw something too," she admitted, trying to ease his mind and convince him to open up.

He took a deep breath, "Okay, yeah. I've seen something outside your bedroom door, more than once. I didn't say anything because I didn't want to scare you. She's shown up on my computer too. At first her name would show up on Discord, requesting to friend me or join a game in Steam. I just ignored it, even thought it might be you messing with me, but things got worse. I'd be in a game and things would glitch out and then there's this girl asking for my help. None of my friends could see it, just me. It was beyond sketch."

More than once? Didn't want to scare her? She tried to temper her anger at her brother making this admission now, only after she had to drag it out of him. She'd had to endure sleepless nights being taunted by nightmares, the humiliating night spent on their parents' couch, the ladybugs, officially self-declaring FaceTime off-limits, all of it. She had believed she alone was experiencing visits from the missing girl.

"What did you see?" she asked.

"A girl. She looks like the girl in the news story, Laura Combs. Sometimes when I'm done brushing my teeth at night, she is standing in the hall looking at your door. Not gonna lie, it freaks me out. I close my eyes and when I open them, *bam!* she's gone. I should have said something before now, but seriously, what would I say? 'Hey Haze, you got a new friend who comes over, in a town where we know no one, during a pandemic, unannounced? Do Mom and Dad know? You should introduce her. And what's up with her poofing?' Who would believe me?"

"I believe you because I've seen her too. But only once outside my room. Well, on my phone too, in a SnapChat filter. It was weird. Oh, and she crashed a FaceTimeing sesh with Mir." She decided to give her brother a little more. "I ran to Mom and Dad's room and slept on their couch."

Holden lost it. Through his laughter he said, "And here I always thought I was the weaker twin."

It was nice to laugh, even if it was over the most absurd thing imaginable. The two hadn't shared a secret since they were in the fifth grade. Hazel couldn't remember what the secret was, but she was certain it was something incredibly scandalous, like who they were crushing on. She would have never thought they would be laughing over seeing a ghost in their hallway during a global pandemic. But she was glad to have this moment of ... normalcy seemed like the wrong word, but that's what it was. It was a normal moment with her twin. He grabbed her head and gave her a normal noogie.

"Stop it!" She feigned injury and halfheartedly tried to pull away.

In the kitchen, with her back turned away from the

construction zone outside, Mom listened to their laughter. It was her favorite sound, one she hadn't heard in months. It was almost therapeutic. She didn't know what they were talking about, and she didn't care. Just to hear them being kids made her realize the toll the past few months had taken on them all. First the pandemic, then the move, the loss of Bailey, all the baffling events and now the terrifying experience with the pool. Nothing had been right for a long time. The family had done their best to remain hopeful, knowing they were in a far better situation than many. Hearing the laughter of her children gave her a sense of peace and calm and a renewed hope that better days were to come. She closed her eyes and listened.

The presence heard the laughter. It missed laughter. A dire situation for those it loved had pushed it to this point. Now the presence felt hopeful as well. Changes were coming, and the presence knew the changes would lead to good things—relief, peace, and calm. Wrongs would be righted. It was only a matter of time now. A very short time.

Although the Oklahoma summer was doing exactly what every Oklahoman expected it to do, the team employed by Sunscapes were on the job, seemingly unaffected by the blistering sun and unrelenting humidity of late summer.

The family stood at the large sliding door upstairs in the not-yet-completed theater room to get the best view of the groundbreaking. An excavator stood at the far end of the yard, a dump truck nearby ready to haul off the excess dirt. The long arm of the machine reached forward, piercing the red earth. The family cheered, and Mom and Dad clinked their coffee mugs together. None of them noticed the presence that manifested behind them. Looking over their shoulders was a thirteen-year-old girl. She had waited thirty-six long and lonely years for this very moment.

Alek Vander stood watching intently while he relished the iced coffee in his thermos. He was spotting the excavator who really didn't need a spotter—Val Meyhan had been at this job since Alek had been in diapers. She knew what she was doing, but rules were rules, so he watched and savored the chilled brew, one of the perks of dating a barista. As Val lifted another load of dirt, he spotted something in the bucket.

He almost wrote it off as a branch or a root, but when the sun caught the object, he realized it couldn't be a root—roots weren't blue and didn't wear clothes. At least, it looked like clothes to him. Maybe it was nothing, but it warranted inspection before they moved forward. He had a hunch, a feeling that whatever it was should not be ignored.

Silently acknowledging to himself that he would likely be the butt of many jokes for weeks to come, he yelled, "Stop! Stop the digging!"

Val was in the groove, as she liked to put it, and wasn't happy about her momentum being broken. She loved the job, and knew she was one of the best. She didn't know why this youngster was interrupting her progress.

"This better be good," she hollered down.

"Lower the boom if you don't mind, Val. Sorry, but something caught my eye."

She was irritated. Alek could already hear his crew's laughter as they mocked him for halting a dig to treasure hunt.

Val expertly lowered the bucket to the ground. As Alek approached, he knew his instinct was right. Sitting on top of the dirt he saw the blue item that had caught his eye. It was a watch, and there were definitely clothes. The watch and clothes were attached to what he believed was a human arm bone.

Alek dropped his thermos, ice and coffee spilling over his boots. He took several steps back, his mouth opening and closing but no sound coming out as his mind searched for words.

His coworker, Jimmy Glass, had taken the borrowed time to check his Facebook page but glanced up and forgot about how many likes the picture of his cat had gotten. Tucking his phone into his pocket, he started to make his way to the boom. When he saw Alek's reaction, he picked up the pace. Jimmy stopped short when he saw the shocking sight the bucket held.

"Val, we need to put this project on hold. Call the boss!" yelled Jimmy, waving up to his coworker.

Val killed the engine and hopped down. She could see the alarm in her younger cohorts and wanted to get things checked out so they could get back to work. She was certain she could get things sorted and back on track without a call to the project leader. The temperature was only going to keep rising, after all. Pulling a bandanna from her back pocket, she wiped sweat from her face and approached the bucket.

"Like I said, this better be ..." She stopped, a chill coming over her as the sweat dripping down her back turned cold. This would definitely warrant a call to the boss, but first she was calling 9-1-1.

From the window, the family was confused by the activity below.

"Oh, come on, don't tell me there's trouble already," Dad said worriedly.

"I wonder what's up," said Mom.

As the family turned to head downstairs and check on the project, the fifth spectator faded away. Her presence was no longer needed.

TWENTY-FOUR

When the call came in to the Stillwater Sheriff's Department, there was some discussion as to who should handle it. Skeletal remains weren't exactly an emergency. Besides, the bones might not actually be human.

Deputy Craig Mitchell volunteered to go take a look. He had been a rookie under Sheriff Reed before the sheriff's retirement and was a Stillwater native. His sister Cami had been one of Laura's classmates. He and his sister grew up in the aftermath of Laura's disappearance, when parents grew more watchful and the town held its breath in fear, small town innocence shaken to its core.

His father spent days with the search party while his mother cooked and delivered meals to the searchers. Cami asked endless questions about where Laura could have gone, and whether she was all right. His parents had done their best to assure her that Laura was fine, and she'd be home someday soon. Young Craig saw the fear in the questioning glances they exchanged as they tried to ease his sister's mind. The reality dawned on him that his parents were lying to them, possibly for the first time.

The cold blast of his cruiser's air conditioning did little to cool the heat he felt as one phrase repeated itself in his mind. *The caller says it appears to be an arm bone, and it was still wearing a watch, a blue watch.*

As he turned into Camelot Crossing, there was little doubt in his mind someone had found the long-missing girl. By the time he arrived on the scene, the Weizaks had been informed by Val Meyhan that something disturbing had been found during their dig, and she had contacted authorities.

"You folks can wait inside the house. I'll keep you posted," she said, before walking toward the deputy's car that was crossing the bridge.

Dad held Mom up, and her face had drained of all color. He guided her into the living room and eased her down onto the couch.

"Mom? Dad? What's wrong? What's going on?" Hazel asked.

The two were silent as Mom sat shaking her head. Hazel's confusion increased the longer they went without speaking. The quiet was finally broken when Mom whispered, "It's horrible."

"What? What is so horrible?" Holden asked.

"They think they've found a human bone," Dad said, sitting down next to Mom, pulling her close to him as she started to cry.

He didn't have the chance to elaborate as he was interrupted by the doorbell. "Stay with your mom," said Dad, getting up to answer.

The three sat stunned, listening to the murmur of Dad's conversation with the deputy. Mom continued to sob quietly. Dad returned a short time later.

"He's going to confirm it is human and if it is, our land will be a crime scene."

Mom's sobs grew deeper, and she buried her head in Holden's shoulder. Hazel got up and Dad followed her over to the window. They watched as Val took the sheriff deputy to the site. He motioned for her to step back and pulled his radio off his belt.

It was quickly determined that the bone was human. From that point on, their lives became something out of a television crime show. A never-ending caravan of official vehicles filled the expansive horseshoe driveway, and their property was strung with police tape. While none of them were considered suspects, they were all interviewed. Thankfully, they never had to leave their home. The agents and officials were respectful, wore masks, and stayed as distant as possible while performing the functions necessary to do a thorough investigation.

Agents from The Oklahoma State Medical Examiner's Office, the Oklahoma State Bureau of Investigation, and the Payne County Sheriff's Department worked around the clock. The night sky was lit up by large, intrusive lights, making it seem as if the sun never set. The curtains stayed drawn, but they weren't enough to block the unnatural light and the relentless sounds, the horror of what was unfolding in the backyard. It was an unspoken given that the body being unearthed had to be that of Laura Combs.

News crews circled like vultures waiting to swoop down on their prey. Reporters stood wired for sound in hopes they might get a word out of an official, or better yet, catch a resident of the house of nightmares. The Weizaks avoided the press, but worried that their home would be seen by so many people under such horrible circumstances. They faced the sad reality that they and their home would become synonymous with such a dreadful thing.

There was no more running on the stairs, and the discovery of the body seemed to lay to rest some of the questions that had plagued their minds. The message on Hazel's wall, Alexa's urgings to check the pool, even the swarm of ladybugs now made sense, sort of. Not so much in a practical way, but they were clues contrived by the girl, somehow, from somewhere. Many unanswered questions still hung in the air; who knew if they would ever be answered?

Each of them dealt with the trauma differently. There were logistical, day-to-day obligations that had to be taken care of, like taking the dogs out, checking the mail and such. Routines were adjusted, and a hold was placed on their mail as they fought to avoid the press, steer clear of investigators, and maintain some sense of anonymity.

Dad immersed himself in work while acting as the contact authorities spoke to regarding progress, next steps, and anything else that was taking place outside. More people arrived, bringing with them new machinery. They put up tents and laid out grids that reached further and further into their yard and the woods. There was always something new every day. He handled it impressively, like a businessman. He held himself and his family together.

While he never broke down, he felt the weight of the situation. Yes, he was devastated at the tragic loss of life and was tormented it had happened so close to the bed where he and his wife slept. He lay awake most nights riddled with guilt for leading the call for his family to choose this place, this house that now held so many frightening memories. He pored over spreadsheets and budgets, wondering what the impact of selling would be. Who would buy it now with all the bad publicity? He hoped he could rally his family to move past this eventually and come to love the house again, and he started budgeting for an exterior remodel. Perhaps a fresh face for the house might make a difference.

Mom grappled with the enormity and the tragedy of the situation. She had taken to sitting in her huge walk-in closet, the thing that brought her so much silly joy just weeks ago. It was the only room in the house without a view of the convoy of official vehicles and press trucks. From there, she also couldn't see the lights and grisly activity taking place in the backyard. She was mourning a child who died thirty-six years ago, one she had never met, and the loss the child's own mother was learning the certainty of just now.

As a mother, she could understand at least some of the devastation. She knew the fear every mother feels when she opens her mind to the horrors the world holds, and the harsh reality of how fragile the thread of fate is that keeps those horrors at bay. That thin thread had snapped in a horrible way, right outside her door. She wasn't sure she could stay after all they had been through, but knew there were heavy consequences if they moved again. It kept her up at night and kept her hiding in her closet, her only refuge from it all.

Holden hid away in his online world, closely connected with his friends who were miles away. At times, he would try to tell them bits and pieces of the story—the parts that could be explained, anyway—but none of them could ever grasp the immensity.

Holden was doing his best to block it all out and pretend it had never happened. He could do that when he was completely immersed in a game of Among Us or Minecraft. It was at night, when he struggled to sleep, that he was back in the pool, the red water gaining on him, the fear pulsing through him as if it were just happening. He had taken to keeping his room stocked with water bottles and snacks and went through his nighttime routine before the sun went down, still fearing he would see the girl in the hallway. He wondered how long these visions would haunt him.

Hazel found freedom even while still confined to the interior of the house. The nightmares ceased, and though her painting supplies had been delayed by the mail hold, the words on her wall faded to the point one would never have known they had been there.

She FaceTimed Miren daily without fear. Most of their conversations now focused on the impending start of a new school year and what that might look like as the virus was showing no mercy. The girls were maturing even as time slowed and the world stood still. They found themselves talking more about civil unrest, the environment, political ideology, and the need for change on so many fronts. Idle chatter of boys and back-to-school wardrobes tethered them to the normal they would likely never know again.

Everyone was dealing with their own immense change. The world was foreign to all in ways no one would have ever believed just months ago. The fear was as palpable as hope. The hope was as desperately needed as change. The Weizaks could never fault anyone with not understanding that what they had experienced was a bit more of an unusual summer of 2020 than many others had endured. Everyone would have a story of that extraordinary year. Who was to say their stories were more incredible than the next person's?

TWENTY-FIVE

THEN

Laura and Momma were a team.

"It's the two of us against the world, baby girl," Momma always said.

While they didn't have much, they had each other. It was more than Momma ever had growing up. When Momma was abandoned by her own parents as an infant, an aunt had taken her in, but that didn't last long. Her aunt wanted to get married and start a family of her own. She didn't need her brother's mistake trailing her through life, making things more complicated. Momma was too young to remember being handed back over to the state. By that time, she was at the age most considered too old to be adopted, even though she hadn't started school yet. It seemed no one wanted a kid born to abusive drug addicts. Momma was shuffled around from one home to another and began a fruitless search for a family who would love her like she was their own.

Laura's imagination was a force. Maybe that's what helped the quiet thirteen-year-old ignore the isolation of living too far from the Stillwater neighborhoods where a walk outside your door meant a day filled with endless possibilities in the company of a friend. They lived outside of town, on the back acre of the Dark Horse Ranch in an old, but clean, trailer. Dark Horse Ranch was owned by the Childers, a loving couple who took Momma and Laura in. They were the closest thing to family either had ever known.

Considered by most to be quite a loner, Laura was more than content with her life in Stillwater. The town was perfect as far as she was concerned. Of course, it was all she had ever known. She loved all its traditions: the fanfare of the homecoming Walkaround at the university to the excitement of downtown's annual Crazy Days, Fall Festival, and tree lighting traditions.

Stillwater thrived on football, and while Laura wasn't a big fan, she would tag along to the high school games with Mr. Childers and his son. One of her favorite town traditions was Senior Circle, which took place every year at Hamilton Field when the clock ran out on the last high school home game.

She loved to watch the graduating class fulfill their rite of passage as Pioneers. There was something magical about the sea of tiny flames from hundreds of lighters that mirrored the night's sky when the stadium lights were dimmed. The soon-to-be graduating class would sway in the dark to the music, songs of their days gone past. Each tune was thoughtfully selected and full of nostalgia and optimism. Her chin would quiver as she fought back tears while the seniors hugged and shared tearful sentiments, mascara running down the girls' faces as tattoos of sadness.

Momma could never go to the football games with them on account of work, but she had been in that circle herself, not that long ago. She didn't know at the time what the world would bring her, nor did she cry like the rest of her classmates. Her sights were set on something bigger than Senior Circle, prom, or even graduation. She turned eighteen before she got her diploma from what was then known as C.E. Donart High School, and aged out of foster care. The day came when she was no longer a stranger in other's homes by the spring of 1970, when she walked across the stage in the school's gymnasium to accept her diploma. She didn't know it yet, but Laura was already growing inside her belly. Laura's daddy couldn't attend the ceremony, so there was no one to cheer for her when she crossed the stage in the royal blue gown with the paper mortar pinned into her feathered hair.

Momma and Daddy had a shotgun wedding and settled in a tiny apartment, waiting for the birth of their child. He filled her head with promises: a piece of land, a house, and a barn where they'd make their living boarding horses and giving riding lessons. The vision of that future flashed before her clenched eyes as she let out a scream and pushed their daughter into the world. She finally felt whole as she held Laura, a wiggling, rooting infant who had a raspy cry. At long last she was a member of a family.

For some time, that wholeness allowed her to overlook her husband's many vices. It came as a shock to her when he left.

"I'm running up to Tiger Drug for some smokes. Need anything?" he said casually one afternoon.

The last thing she ever said to him was, "Nothing I can think of."

When he hadn't returned two hours later, she noticed all his belongings had been cleared out. She'd always wonder if he would've come home had she said she needed some milk or a loaf of bread and kicked herself for not needing anything that day.

He'd spent all their savings and sold off everything of value before that day to pay off his gambling debts. His truck was in her name, as were a couple of ill-gotten charge cards he had maxed out. She was a single mother of a three-year-old, in debt over her head, so broke she couldn't make the next month's rent.

Mr. Childers took pity on her and gave her a full-time job at The Roadside Motel where she'd been working part-time cleaning the guest rooms. He also let her move into the empty trailer sitting on his ranch.

Laura and Momma never talked about Daddy and because of that, Laura's memory of him had become more faded than the few snapshots of the man that were kept in a worn and cracked photo album. Laura didn't ask about him much because she knew Momma didn't like talking about him. She learned at a young age that the mention of Daddy could bring tears to Momma's eyes. Laura never wanted to see Momma cry, so she kept quiet. The hazy tatters of memories of her daddy were woven with musings from her imagination, leaving her with a skewed vision of the man and unable to reconcile her recall with the reality of his abandonment.

While Laura didn't talk about Daddy, she did think about him often. She made up stories in her head about where he was, what he was doing, when he'd come back. When thoughts of Daddy touched her mind, her hand would make its way to the small of her back. She and Daddy had matching birthmarks in the same spot—left side, too low for most to see. While she liked the idea of sharing something with him, it served as a reminder that he was gone. She couldn't escape the fact that she hadn't been good enough for him. Why had he left her? It wasn't long before those unanswered questions soured her feelings about him. He grew farther and farther from her heart as idolization eroded into resentment.

Aside from the birthmark that no one really ever saw, Laura and her Momma were the spitting image of each other. They had the same long, dirty brown hair that held a hint of curl, more frizz than curl on days when the humidity hit 80%, which in Oklahoma was most days. They looked at the world with the same piercing green eyes and their crooked-toothed smiles were punctuated by matching dimples on their right cheek.

Laura never knew how much these similarities meant to Momma; to have someone who shared her looks and her mannerisms. A career foster child with no known siblings, she had always felt alone in the world. That void was filled the moment Laura had taken her first breath.

Momma worked two jobs, and that meant Laura was left on her own much of the time. She didn't mind because she wasn't really alone. The Childers' Border Collie, Rex, was always by her side.

Mr. Childers would laugh and say, "Seems Rex here wasn't cut out for shepherding cattle. He'd much rather trek around these woods with you than work for me."

He was right—Rex was usually right beside Laura whether she was lost in a book, daydreaming in the tire swing, or exploring the red dirt trails that branched in every direction from the Dark Horse Ranch.

She didn't have any close friends. There were kids at school she ate lunch with and hung out with at recess, but most of them lived in town and most had a momma and a daddy.

Laura liked school and was a good student who always got good grades. Her report cards bore remarks such as *Courteous, Hardworking,* and *A pleasure to have in class.* School work didn't always come easy to her, especially math, but she tried hard. Her favorite teacher was Mrs. Spencer, because she suggested books to her during library block and wrote nice things at the top of her work, like *Lovely imagery!* and *Beautiful prose!* Laura had to look up the word *prose;* she liked looking words up. Her cheeks flushed with pride when Mrs. Spencer wrote, *Keep this up and you will be a writer someday!* on one of her essays.

Laura loved animals and took care of the barn cats that didn't really need taking care of. She named them all, even the ones too skittish to allow her to approach. She made sure she knew which cat was expecting a litter, so she could keep a close eye out and make sure the kittens were birthed in a safe place. But she also knew the ranch could be a harsh world for the little barn kittens and sometimes the runt or even a whole litter didn't survive. Laura dug resting places for all that didn't make it and placed small stone markers on the top of each grave. She picked wildflowers and lay them at each site as well.

The ranch hands would let her know if they found an injured barn cat. She would track the cat down and sit with it, petting and whispering comforting words while it went through the process of passing. She never wanted them to be alone in their final hours. Her soft heart left her saddened by every loss, even if she just discovered a quitter while candling eggs in the chicken coop.

Her favorite thing on the ranch was watching calvings. Emotion filled her while she quietly cheered for each new life as it rose on shaky legs and took its first steps.

Dark Horse Ranch was a Cow-Calf farm. She tried not to think of what happened to the calves when they left the ranch. Once she asked Mr. Childers why he named a cattle farm Dark Horse Ranch. There were a few horses on the ranch—every ranch had at least a few horses—but she thought it was funny that a cattle ranch was named after horses.

He laughed for a good long time and said, "Because no one expected a jackass like me to become a success."

Laura laughed too, even though she didn't get the joke and still didn't understand why a cattle ranch was called Dark Horse Ranch.

TWENTY-SIX

Momma carved out time every Saturday for Laura. They would go to town for errands and a little fun. Laura would turn the radio up, and they would sing along to the songs on K105 during their drive, laughing the whole time. Momma loved their Saturday outings as much as Laura did, and while she had fun treating her daughter as a youngster, she came to enjoy that time even more as Laura grew from a curious child into a creative teenager. She marveled at her fortune and felt pride and contentment with every moment she spent with her daughter. Momma wished she could give Laura more, but knew the value of her time and love. Laura never complained; the young girl seemed to treasure the very same things she did.

Their first stop was always the library, where Laura would check out ten books every week, the maximum number allowed. They took turns choosing where they would go for lunch. Laura's favorites were Pop's Root Beer and Bobo's Cantina, but Momma preferred Eskimo Joe's and Mr. Burger. Then they would window-shop at Katz's Department Store, catch a matinee at The Leachman or grab a frozen treat at

Whirla-Whip before doing their grocery shopping at Consumers IGA. They both loved their Saturdays together.

One Saturday while Laura sat in the trailer's tiny kitchen eating a bowl of Frosted Flakes, waiting for Momma to get ready for their outing, Momma said, "I got you something." She slid a watch and two cassette tapes across the green Formica tabletop. "Someone left this stuff at The Roadside. Mr. Childers said we could keep it. I called all the guests who stayed there last weekend, but no one claimed any of it. Thought you might like them. Tears for Fears and Duran Duran. I think you're responsible enough to have your own watch now. It's a nice one, but not my style."

Momma eyeballed the tiny letters stamped on the tapes. "Never heard of either one of them, but thought you might have. Whoever left them behind didn't have the courtesy to leave the cases," she said with a wink.

Momma was always bringing home forgotten items from The Roadside, but the Swatch watch quickly became Laura's favorite. You could only find them in town at The Wooden Nickel, and she was the first of her classmates to have one. Obsessed with the alarm function, she set alarms for everything. It had a bright blue band and a face encircled with flags. Just looking at the watch took her thoughts to setting sail across an ocean to a country she'd only known in books.

While Momma's work at The Roadside Motel was backbreaking—she did everything there from keeping guests happy to keeping the rooms clean—she insisted her second job was the hardest. Every day she clocked out at four in the afternoon and went straight to the ranch house to help with Mrs. Betty Mae Childers.

Miss B, as everyone called her, was Mr. Childers' wife and suffered from a most severe case of Alzheimer's. Although Miss B spent her days and nights in the care of nurses, no one but

Momma could tend to her during what everyone called her sundowners time.

Laura asked how sitting with the kind Miss B could be harder than taking care of a whole motel.

"It's not just a job, sweetie. It's a labor of love," Momma replied.

Miss B always had fondness for Momma. The Childers had lost a baby girl, the infant only breathed life for one hour before passing on in Miss B's arms. They named their baby girl Becca Jean and had she lived, she would be the same age as Momma. Laura thought it was sad that while the Childers mourned the loss of their daughter, Momma's own parents let her slip away from them, unloved and forgotten.

The Childers had planted a tree a year after Becca Jean passed. That tree, a Mossycup White Oak, was giant now. The tire swing, hung by the ranch hands, was Laura's favorite reading spot, Rex's favorite napping spot, and the tree shaded the ranch hands on their breaks.

Most days, taking care of Miss B was a pleasure. Momma would relieve the day nurse and start her shift by trying to coax Miss B into eating a few bites of supper. Miss B didn't eat much anymore and was wasting away to but a slip of her old self. Momma would get her into her night coat and brush her long, silver hair while she sang to her. Miss B was partial to old country songs and church hymns. Then Momma would get Miss B settled into bed and read to her as she fell asleep, not knowing where Miss B's mind might find her when she woke.

On good nights, Momma could catch a few winks in the Laz-E-Boy that sat beside Miss B's hospital bed in the converted sunroom. But other nights, sleep didn't find Miss B and Momma would spend her time trying to comfort her and chase away the ghosts that only existed in Miss B's afflicted mind.

At 11:00 p.m. the night nurse came on, and she and Momma would share a cup of tea while Momma filled her in on how the evening had gone. Both did their best not to wake Miss B, because if they did, she would cry and plead with Momma to stay. On those occasions, it wasn't uncommon for Miss B to call Momma Becca Jean and ask her not to leave again.

If all went well, just before midnight Momma would drag her tired self to her barely running Chevy Nova and make the quarter mile drive over the dirt trail and cattle guard to the trailer. She would open the squeaky door as quietly as possible, tiptoe to the bathroom, brush her teeth, get undressed, and silently slip into bed to catch a few hours of desperately needed sleep before the alarm woke her at 5:30 a.m. and she made her way back to The Roadside Motel.

TWENTY-SEVEN

While Laura was content with her solitary life, Momma had needs that Laura couldn't understand. Momma didn't like being alone and was always chasing after a dream—a home of her own, someone to share her life with, a new Daddy, and little brother or sister for Laura. She wanted to give Laura all the things she herself never had.

A pattern emerged as Momma pursued that dream, and it followed each new man in and out of their lives. Momma would mention a new name in passing and would laugh more, seem happier. On Saturday nights, she would get dressed up and through a haze of perfume and hairspray would tell Laura she was going to dinner at the Steer Inn or dancing at the Tumbleweed. She would spin around to get a thumbs-up from Laura and then plant a kiss on Laura's forehead, leaving behind a pink lip mark and the faint scent of Jovan Musk.

"There's a TV dinner in the freezer. Be sure to turn the oven off when it's done. Don't stay up too late. I'll see you in the morning," Momma fussed. She never reminded Laura about any of those things on weeknights. Laura guessed it made Momma feel less at odds about leaving her on weekends too.

Sunday dinner the following evening usually meant a new "friend" would be introduced to Laura. She did her best to be cordial to Momma's boyfriends, and for the most part they were to her as well. Some she might never see again while others stuck around for a month or so, coming over more often until eventually they were sleeping at the trailer. On those nights, Laura could hear their giggling and whispering through the paper-thin walls. She would pull out her Walkman (compliments of a forgetful guest at The Roadside Inn), and play one of her cassette tapes to quiet the sounds that embarrassed her.

Bubba Floyd entered their lives the same as all the others. He stayed at the motel while working road construction on the interstate. Bubba was a good-looking smooth talker, but wasn't the most reliable worker. He stayed up too late smoking, drinking beer, and playing cards. He had a habit of ignoring the early morning wake-up call from Charlene Watts, who lived in a makeshift apartment at the Roadside. Charlene and her husband, Mark, kept watch over the motel overnight.

After several days of showing up late or not showing up at all, Bubba got fired. By that time, he had been around long enough to fill up a little of that lonely spot in Momma's life, and she was more than willing to allow him to fill up some more. Bubba moved out of The Roadside Motel and into the trailer at the Dark Horse Ranch, bringing the late nights drinking beer and playing cards with his rowdy friends along with him.

Bubba was tall and had a shock of thick, curly hair that was black as coal. His arms bulged with muscles, and his eyes were dark and always sizing people up. He had a mean streak too. His true colors seeped through more and more with each cap he popped off a beer bottle. Momma wasn't always around to see that side of him, but Laura got a glimpse of his demons, try as he might to keep them hidden.

Once again, Momma was turning a blind eye to things she didn't want to see. "I'm no spring chick," she lamented to Charlene. "My biological clock is ticking!"

She was serious; she could hear the *tick-tick-tick* in her head as she looked in the mirror, pulling the skin back around her eyes and her neck. Laura caught her eyeballing the hair dye at the TG&Y during one of their Saturday outings, and for the first time noticed the silver strands in Momma's hair.

Laura grew up with the hard-working Mr. Childers and his ranch hands, and felt Momma's weariness when Sunday rolled around, and she faced the work week ahead. But Bubba had to be the laziest person she'd ever known, so it was no wonder to her when he got fired. The toughest thing he did was pick up the phone every day to call the unemployment people and argue about his benefits. Never once did he help clean up around the trailer or do any tasks that might make life easier, like oiling the squeaky doors, or fixing the leak in the bathroom sink. Laura thought he should be helping out and looking for work instead of kicking back watching TV and eating the food Momma worked hard to buy.

Bubba was a different person around Momma. As soon as she walked into the trailer, he would turn on the charm, telling her how pretty she was. He talked sweet to her, complimented her cooking and was always nice to Laura when she was home. But on nights that Momma worked, Laura got home from school to find Bubba on the couch, yelling at a game show with at least three or four of what he called "empty soldiers" lined up on the coffee table and hours to line up more before Momma got home. Laura guessed that was the reason why Mr. Childers said Bubba was a wolf in sheep's clothes.

Bubba had secrets he was hiding from everyone. The court-appointed anger management classes taught him ways to bite back his temper. The psycho-babbling social worker gave him techniques that helped keep his anger in check, most times. He'd come a long way from the days when his fists balled up the second his pulse quickened, releasing his red rage on what-ever was closest—a wall, a woman, a window, a do-goodie in a bar who made the mistake of crossing him. Bubba knew when to cut bait, and he knew his current situation, jobless and living off a single mom with wedding bells in her eyes, was not ideal. But he knew enough to enjoy it while it lasted. It was a comfy place where he could lay low and wait for his unemployment benefits. He'd know when the time came to bail.

TWENTY-EIGHT

Mr. Childers was what Momma called "getting up there in years." Laura knew that was a nicer way of saying he was getting old. The ranch was becoming too much for him, and his son Thomas had proven he had no intentions of taking over the family business. He'd passed the bar exam and was moving to Texas with his young wife, who was expecting their first child.

Mr. Childers had doubts about his ability to keep his beloved wife safe at home as her condition worsened. He had gone so far as to look into some nursing homes and found that they weren't cheap. There was also the fear that Miss B would not take to a new environment and deteriorate faster. But he kept the idea in his back pocket and started thinking of ways to fund the move if need be.

The college was growing and more people were moving to Stillwater every day. Some of those people wanted big, new houses. Mr. Childers saw the opportunity and started selling off some of his land. The first big parcel was to the south of the ranch. As soon as the ink dried on the deed, developers started working that land to build large homes. The name of the new neighborhood that was once hunting ground for Mr. Childers and his cohorts was Camelot Crossing.

The face of the terrain changed almost overnight. Laura was drawn to the site, with its steady hammer heartbeat and growling machines that took on a rhythm when paired with the shouts of dozens of workers and the country music they listened to as they built something from nothing on the newly tamed land. The homes were huge; she was pretty sure they were mansions. She meandered through the woods every day just to visit the development.

One house, the third one going up, reminded her of something from a fairy tale. It was a mix of brick and stone and cream-colored stucco held together with dark, wooden beams. It had to be unlike any other house in Stillwater. After crossing a wooden bridge, a cobblestone walk led to the huge front door that had a small hatch instead of a peephole. It was all very medieval and amazing. The chimney stretched toward the sky and was topped off by double stacks that looked like enormous chess pieces. The most awe-inspiring feature was the large stained-glass window at the entrance. She had only ever seen stained glass on churches, never on a house.

She imagined the people who would live in such a fantastical house, and even wondered what it would be like to live there herself. In her mind, she spun a tale of a man for Momma who was good and kind, who would welcome them and build a family. In her mind, she could see all of Momma's dreams coming true. She could picture the man, who smoked a fragrant pipe instead of smelly cigarettes. He had close-cropped hair and graying sideburns, and wore wire-rimmed glasses and sweater vests. The magical house was the perfect backdrop for the wedding in her fabled story.

She found a book at the library and learned that the house was built in the Tudor style. The house and its architecture led her down the rabbit hole of Tudor times, reading of war and plague, lords and ladies, child kings and knights, beheadings and famine. It was a time when leaders were feared for their ever-shifting beliefs and the gray air was thick and choking from coal fires and poor sanitation.

How different things were now. The person building the third house in Camelot Crossing had taken a piece of this frightful past and built it here in a beautiful setting, where the air was fresh and clear, medicine had an answer for most maladies, and life was safe and peaceful.

TWENTY-NINE

Spring was usually Laura's favorite time of year. But the spring of 1984 brought more leaden storm clouds than sunny days, and the strong winds carried with them changes that would alter the lives of all who called Dark Horse Ranch home.

Bubba became more brooding and demanding as his buddies came around less. Without the distraction of friends and poker, his drinking got worse instead of better. Miss B was taking a change for the worse, as well. She saw fewer moments of clarity as disease ravaged her fragile mind. Momma succumbed further to Bubba's charms and took to apologizing for Bubba's moods as her grip tightened on the flawed man and the belief she could mold him into the image of her dreams.

Bubba fell back into old patterns and his anger fell upon the closest target, which was Laura. Most days she could hide away from his angry tirades by staying outside until the sun went down, then laying low in her bedroom until he passed out. If weather kept her inside, she did her best to become invisible. She even tried to block out his drunken laughter with her Walkman. The Tears for Fears tape Momma found at The

Roadside was her favorite. The songs were angry and sad and moody. There were two songs she liked the most: "Memories Fade" and "Mad World," because their lyrics stirred emotion in her like nothing ever had.

Momma was spending more time tending to Miss B and usually found Bubba passed out on the couch by the time she got home. In her overworked, exhausted state, she didn't pay heed to his rapid slip down the steep slope into heavier drinking and darker behavior. Laura kept quiet because she could see the burden of Miss B's decline in Momma's eyes and didn't want to add to her troubles. As long as Laura kept her head down and avoided him, she could usually prevent riling him up. But sometimes something as silly as shutting the door too hard, or not twisting a lid back on a pop bottle to his liking, could set him off.

Monday, April 9th started off like any Monday. Momma woke Laura and fixed breakfast while the two said their good mornings and discussed their day, doing their best to ignore Bubba's loud snores just feet away on the sofa. As Laura gathered her belongings to head up to her bus stop, Momma warned of her incoming storms and told her to grab her jacket. Laura was reaching for the door before she remembered she needed lunch money. She went to the jar where Momma kept her tip money from guests at The Roadside. She pulled out a ten and noticed the old Mason jar was almost empty, confirming her suspicions that Bubba was helping himself to the money.

Though she was already late, she paused long enough for an embrace from Momma, who held on a beat longer than usual and whispered, "I love you," before planting a kiss on the top of her head. Laura wiggled free and bounded out the door, hollering back, "Love you too!" as she ran down the red dirt path, eager to start the new day and not miss the bus.

The day passed as any other. She was happy to see she got

a 94% on her algebra exam. At lunch, she sat with her friend, Cami, and the two gossiped about the new boy who they both agreed was super cute. On the bus ride home, she watched the dark clouds roll in, blotting out the sun. Bus 17 pushed against strong winds that whistled through the bus's windows and turned empty fields into Martian landscapes, with red dirt devils spinning into existence, dancing wildly for a few brief moments before dying out.

Mr. Childers and Rex were waiting at the front gate of the ranch in the farm truck to give Laura a ride to the trailer. As they bumped over the cattle guard, large drops of rain broke free of the clouds, sounding like they would punch holes through the roof of the old Studebaker.

The sky released the full force of the storm as she gave Rex a final scratch behind the ear and hopped down from the passenger seat. She turned and waved to Mr. Childers from the top of the cement stairs and was startled by a loud clap of thunder. Her tan jacket was polka-dotted with rain drops as a gust of wind caught the door and yanked it from her grasp with a loud bang.

Mr. Childers was driving away and didn't hear Bubba howl, "Hell's bells, girl! You trying to wake the dead?" as she crossed the threshold. Laura said nothing in reply—there was nothing to say. Bubba already had five dead soldiers lined up on the coffee table, and she spied a couple more that had fallen to the floor.

He got up and stumbled a few steps. Laura cowered as he passed by her on the way to the fridge. He grabbed another beer. A piece of paper was clenched in his hand. He set it on the kitchen table as he popped the lid off the beer, then snatched the paper back up and shook it in her face as she tried to slink away to her bedroom.

"Ya know what dis is?" he slurred, spilling beer on her

Members Only jacket. She fought back hot tears that burned her eyes as he proceeded to tell her.

"A le'er from da' Unempoinmt Scurty Commshun."

He was almost incomprehensible, but Laura got the gist. She saw the word *Denied* shouting in red letters from the top of the paper. Bubba pushed past her to make his way back to the worn couch, where he fell back rather than sat, all the while mumbling and cursing under his breath. Laura took the moment to make her escape.

In her bedroom, she closed the door and locked it for the first time in her life. She leaned against the door trying to calm her breath and noticed an unopened bottle of New York Seltzer (black cherry, her favorite) on her bedside table. It wouldn't be cold, but it would be better than nothing to tide her over till he passed out. She was shivering more from fear than cold, and stripped her damp clothes off, changing into dry jeans and her favorite sweatshirt. She fumbled through a drawer to find the matching socks—the set had been a gift from the Childers last Christmas. The sweatshirt and fuzzy socks were covered in a ladybug print.

She had just turned the page to chapter two of her newest library find, *The Door in the Wall*, when Bubba started pounding on her door. The knock was so abrupt and loud that she almost fell off her bed. She held her breath until he finally spoke.

"Get out here'n fix me sumthin to eat!" His voice boomed louder and angrier than the growing storm.

She had never cooked dinner for him and knew no matter what she did, he wouldn't be satisfied. In a panic she stumbled over her thoughts, and words were lost to her. Outside her door he grew inpatient, his pounding shaking the walls.

"Ya hear me girl?"

He was trying to open the door now, the knob dancing as he

tried to force his way in. The air inside the trailer was more unstable than the storm, and she was filled with a sense of dread. She believed her only option was to run, so she grabbed her rain boots and jacket. The jacket was still a little wet and now stunk of bitter beer and Bubba's breath, but she didn't want to take the time to search for her raincoat. She waved her hand blindly under the bed until it touched on the flashlight she hid there to read after Momma called lights out. Bubba was still hollering and pounding on the door when she raised her window and made the short leap to the rain-soaked ground below.

She hit the ground running and made a dash to the tree line. Her terrified mind blinded her rationale with what-ifs. She lucked upon a deer trail and ran full force, escaping the weather and Bubba's grasp.

Bubba kept pounding on the door to the room for some time after Laura made her escape out the window. The roar of uncontrollable fury filled his ears, and the electrifying buzz threatened to overcome his ability to let it slide.

He gave up on the idea of a hot meal courtesy of the girl. His stomach now threatened to turn on him if he didn't put something besides low-brow beer in it. Bubba stumbled to the kitchen and threw together a sandwich of bologna, white bread, and a squirt of mustard. Before collapsing into his well-worn spot on the couch, he grabbed a can of Cheez Ballz, foregoing another brew for a Mountain Dew.

The food calmed his blood and his stomach, and he started thinking of how he would explain this to the brat's mom. He wasn't planning on staying around much longer, but this setback, compliments of the unemployment folks, was going to delay his exit. As he tapped the orange dust remnants of the cheese snack into his open mouth, he decided to try to make amends with the kid.

He knocked softly on her door and tempered his voice as he called her name. Heat rose in his cheeks when, after several knocks and calls, she had not replied. Bubba tried the knob again and remembered she had locked it. How dare she? That realization brought fire to his face.

His anger grew as he raised his hand to the top of the door trim and fruitlessly groped about, searching for a key. If he knew anything, he knew how to jimmy one of these flimsy locks. He went to the tiny bathroom and pulled out the drawer under the sink, spilling its contents across the cracked linoleum floor. His vision was growing blurry with rage, but he spotted a bobby pin, plucked it from the scattered mess and headed back for the door, slipping on the tube of toothpaste, flattening it and squeezing its contents over the littered space.

It took no longer than a minute for the cylinder to release with a click. The door pulled sharply inward into the room as the pressure from the open window snatched it out of his grasp. Pink curtains flapped limply under the weight of the soaking rain. She was gone.

There was no way to say his piece and hide this from her momma now. All his attempts to extinguish his fury flew out the open window. He slammed back through the house, put on his boots and his slicker, grabbed a beer, and burst out of the trailer. Bubba yelled into the storm, "Girl, just wait till I find you!"

THIRTY

Laura came to a seizing halt, her lungs threatening to burst should she not slow everything down. She saw a twinkling light through the trees ahead so she pushed on, following its glow, and soon found herself staring at the back of her fairy tale house. She was seeing the back of the property for the first time, and even with a thick, dark sky she immediately recognized it.

An outside lamp left on shone directly over a door that rattled in the wind, past the massive pit and the stone walkway, at the back of the house. A bolt of lightning shoved her forward, headlong into the door carelessly left ajar. A jolt of electricity abuzz nearby warned of another flash, closer, an instant before it struck. She rushed inside, never giving pause to second-guess her actions.

She found herself in the garage and went directly to the closest door, opening it without considering that it might be locked, or what might be on the other side. She slid off her muddy boots before entering what was a large utility room. Having made it this far, she had to press on, seizing upon the chance to see the inside of the beautiful home.

Amazed by the smell of its newness, her fingers traced over leaded glass cabinets that lined the adjoining hall. Her heart raced as she absorbed every detail of every room, becoming more at ease and brave with each step. Rooms that were bigger than her whole home and were more done up than a castle were revealed in the glare of her flashlight. Everything from massive chandeliers to the oddly shaped doorways that mirrored the shape of stained-glass window. The window and doorways were not square, not arched, but pointed at the top. The room with the stained-glass window was lined in dark, shiny wood shelves that reached halfway up its high walls. A balcony was above her, reaching out over the space, evoking an image of a lovelorn princess or star-crossed lovers.

Her pulse quieted and fear was forgotten as she dared to explore the upstairs, shining the flashlight, as its beam was swallowed up by the massive staircase. Again she found room after room of magazine-worthy décor, more bathrooms than she could believe any family would ever need. The passing of time was lost to her as she entered a room that was beyond her imagination.

Delicate crystals dangled from the fixture in the middle of the ceiling, throwing prisms onto the walls in the flashlight beam. She followed the edge of the room, stopping to inspect the milky colored wallpaper before placing her entire hand on the wall, sliding it across the swirls highlighted not by color, but by texture. It was fuzzy, like a well-worn blanket. At the angle where the wall covering ended, an amazing story began—a mural spanned before her. A meadow, a fawn drinking from a babbling brook, trees, flowers ... every imaginable creature of the woods under the blue sky. The scene was alive, illuminated by the beam of her light. This was a room to give to a girl who was loved beyond measure, most likely by her father. A father who could bring to life such an amazing gift.

For the first time in her life, she felt the flush of envy, just for a moment, but it passed in a flash. She could have mistaken it for a shiver since her wet clothes had stopped dripping, but clung to her body with a weighty, damp cold.

There was one last room at the end of the long hall. She opened the door to a room that was unexpectedly bright thanks to its wall of windowed doors that looked out over the backyard. Beyond the doors was a vast balcony that stretched below to what she now believed to be a hole for a swimming pool. There it was again, that pulse-quickening shiver. As she tried to decide if she should weather the storm to walk outside onto the balcony, just to see the view, a beeping noise broke through the sounds of the storm. It was her watch—a ten o'clock alarm telling her it was lights out. How had so much time passed?

Unsure of her route, she scanned the room and eyed a half wall, opposite the side on which she had entered. It had to be another stairway, perhaps dropping her close to the garage door. She bolted that direction and almost stepped into air, her forward foot not finding anything on which to land. She grabbed the pony wall before almost losing her grip on the flashlight and falling over the edge. The stairs had not been completed all the way up to the room she was in. Quickly changing course, she plunged down the long hallway and out of the house the way she came in. Almost fleeing through the outside door in her stocking feet, she turned back and crammed her feet into her muddy boots.

The storm had become fiercer as she had given herself a tour of the dreamy house. Tiny rivers had popped up throughout the expanse between the house and the forest. It was like she stepped out into a different world. She spotted a makeshift walkway made of plywood, and she carefully crossed to it, realizing now that her boots were on the wrong feet, making her feel clumsy and off-kilter. There was no time to correct it; she would have to deal with the discomfort.

The planked path lined the edge of the giant swimming pool pit. Foolishly, she took a look over the side to see feet below her a muddy sea churning as the rain pounded the already pooled water. As she turned away from the dizzying view, balancing herself and setting her focus on the forest ahead, she heard something. It sounded like someone was calling her name. She froze. Was that Bubba's voice? Had Momma discovered her missing and sent people out looking for her? She wished she had never left the trailer. How could she ever talk Bubba down from his anger at her for running away, forcing him to go after her in this weather? But was it Bubba?

She stood transfixed, listening for the voice. The only sound she heard was the crash of thunder, and she dropped the flashlight in a flinch caused by the cracking boom. She watched as it banged off the rocky sides of the pit, its light swallowed up by the rising waters at the bottom of the hole.

She tossed her head to fling away her soaked hair and the stream of rain that pelted her eyes as they struggled to adjust to the darkness without her flashlight. Before they could focus, the night lit up again, and she thought she caught a glimpse of something at the edge of the woods. A raspy gasp escaped her as another clap of thunder silenced her scream. She lost her footing, arms circling for a brief, hopeful second before she tumbled over the edge.

She grasped at anything that might stop her descent, her hand seizing on a thick root, boots threatening to fall off as her feet scrambled for footing. Struggling to claw her way back to the top, she looked up to see how far she had to go. Lightning echoed off the water below her, and she saw a figure standing at the top of the pit. She could be saved, and thoughts of getting in trouble had long left her mind as she feared for her safety.

She gathered air in her lungs, choking on rain as she lifted her voice to scream. "Help me!" The root she clung to loosened, and she fell again, hard. The blanket of red stars that flashed before her eyes wasn't caused by lightning and burned out quickly as her world went black.

THIRTY-ONE

That night the thunder woke Miss B with a start. Momma had feared this. Miss B had never liked thunderstorms. She went to Miss B's side and the frail woman grabbed hold of her waist, squeezing her with a strength that was shocking.

Over and over, Miss B repeated the same thing. "I'm so sorry, so, so sorry."

Momma rocked Miss B, shushing her, telling her everything was all right. What neither Momma nor Miss B knew was that nothing would ever be all right again.

Even Rex was disturbed by the storms that night, which was out of character for the amiable dog. The same thunder that woke Miss B startled Rex as he lay curled up next to Mr. Childers while he read the paper in his comfy chair. The dog was growling while he stared out the window, hair on end. Mr. Childers tried to quiet him, then dragged him to the laundry room and shut him in when the dog wouldn't heed his warnings. No one needed to wake his wife up over an armadillo caught out in the storm.

Not until the night nurse showed up, a bit late due to the

ferocity of the rainfall, was Momma able to pull herself away from Miss B's clutches. Still Miss B wailed on, thrashing in ever mounting frenzy from an unknown cause. The night nurse gave Miss B something to help her sleep, and she finally quieted enough that Momma felt comfortable leaving. As Momma reached for her raincoat, Miss B sat up, startling them both.

"Please don't leave so soon, Laura," she said before lying back down and closing her eyes.

Momma buttoned up her coat and looked at the sleeping woman. She whispered, "You get some sleep, Miss B. Everything will be better in the morning."

It wasn't unusual for Miss Betty to mix up names. Momma gave the night nurse a wink and went out into the rain through the back door of the sunroom.

The storm was spent and had calmed to a steady rainfall with an occasional far-off rumble by the time Momma headed home. She was exhausted, as she usually was on Miss Betty's difficult nights and this one had been a doozie. She wasn't pleased at all to find Bubba passed out on the couch. When she saw that he still had his boots on and his feet propped up on the coffee table, she was angered as all get-out.

She walked over to him and nudged his leg with a force that should have woken anyone, but Bubba went right on snoring. With a deep sigh, she bent over to take his boots off. Anger shifted to alarm and confusion when she noticed his boots were caked with mud, which meant her table and her floors were a mess too. She was going to have to find a way to lay down some rules, and he was going to clean up this mess. She wouldn't be satisfied until she could never tell it happened.

Knowing she probably couldn't rouse him in this state and being too tired to pick a fight, she yanked his boots off and put them in the linoleum entry. Bubba barely stirred the whole time. As she passed by him again on her way to the bathroom, she gave him a rough nudge to settle him into a semi-reclined position that she hoped would quiet his heavy snores.

She made her way to the bathroom, paused at Laura's room and considered peeking in on her, but let the thought go. The creaky door might wake her up and besides, there was no need to check on her. She would be quietly breathing the deep breaths of the sleeping. In a sleep-deprived daze, she couldn't find the toothpaste and scrounged through her makeup bag for the mini tube of toothpaste she kept there for reasons she may have learned from *Seventeen* or *Ladies Home Journal,* her favorite magazines in the motel lobby. She couldn't believe she'd let them run out of toothpaste.

Maybe summer would be easier when the students left and took their roadside motel keggers with them. Summers were always slower in Stillwater. She brushed her teeth, got undressed and quietly slipped into her bed to catch a few hours of sleep before the alarm woke her at five-thirty in the morning.

THIRTY-TWO

Tuesday, April 10th found Stillwater, Oklahoma waking up to a muggy day that only promised to get muggier. It also found Harry Buhl way behind schedule. There hadn't been much call for new pools in town until the new neighborhood out south started being developed. The builders wanted a swimming pool on nearly every lot. He welcomed the windfall for his previously struggling business, Buhl's Pools, but now the notorious spring weather had sent Harry's backlog spiraling out of control. Throw in some poor hiring practices, like taking on his wife's cousin Trevor, who had zero skills and not an ounce of work ethic, and the poorly timed (but minor, thankfully) back injury of his right-hand man James Wheeler, and he wasn't sure how he was ever going to get caught up.

Harry had started cutting corners he had always promised he would never cut. But the builders were calling constantly, demanding faster turnaround times. It was time for his business to sink or swim, pun intended. Now they were calling all day, leaving angry tirades which his wife scrawled out on a message pad, time-stamped and dated, and stacked neatly in a pile on the side-table by his recliner.

With the pressure of the workload and the backlog weighing on his mind, and no inkling of the previous night's events, he and his flatbed set out, both burdened with a day and a half worth of work. He was hoping the unreliable Trevor might show up at some point to help him out.

His first task was to correct a massive blunder made by Trevor at the third house going up in Camelot Crossing. He was miserable thinking of the time that would be lost refilling six feet of depth of what was to be a play pool, not a diving one. It was back-breaking work, just ask James Wheeler. Trevor had not found his calling in the heavy task. James Wheeler always said, "It's an art. It really is." In the pool excavating art, Trevor was painting with the wrong kind of brush.

Harry was the only contractor on the muddy mess of a site. The conditions would make this job precarious, but it had to be done before progress could be made. He should set up a pump and drain the pit before putting dirt back in. The right thing to do was to get a truckload or two of extra soil to stabilize the area, but he took a gamble, sparing a fair amount of thought, before admitting to himself he would have to make things work even while cutting corners he wished he didn't have to cut. More of his precious time was wasted shuffling around all manner of equipment left too close to the perimeter of the dig.

He nearly slid right into the pit, cursing the sloppy crew, Trevor, his wife, and everything else that led him to this moment. He turned his back on the mess to unload his Bobcat, and something at the bottom of the pit caught his eye—a flicker of reflected sunlight. With a guilty sigh he turned his back on the sight that, for safety's sake, should be checked out. Rolling the dice again, he ignored that voice in his head. Had Harry taken the time to investigate, the story of Laura Combs' whereabouts would have been told much differently.

When the job was finished, he directed his mind to the many more tasks ahead and told himself he wouldn't cut corners on the next pool, on his honor. As he crossed the bridge, heading to the next site, which he was overseeing himself this time, his untrustworthy and hopefully temporary companion, Trevor, blew right by him in his beat-up Plymouth Fury. Trevor's sun-baked arm hung out the window, and some hair band was wailing from his beefed-up speakers. Harry tapped the horn on his truck, but Trevor took no notice. The only person Harry had to help him out was two hours late and heading in the opposite direction of where he was needed. Harry almost laughed to himself, but couldn't muster the energy, saving all he had for the long day ahead.

THIRTY-THREE
THE TIME BETWEEN THEN AND NOW

Charlotte Combs had led a lonely life. From the moment she was born until the moment she became a mother, she didn't belong to anyone. She couldn't help but feel cursed when the one thing that gave her purpose and made her feel whole had disappeared. She was driven by a maddening mix of hope, despair, grief, and remorse. If it weren't for Mr. Childers nudging her forward, always knowing the right thing to do, to learn and know more about Laura's disappearance, she would probably still be lying in her bed wishing it all was a bad dream. He propped her up, despite all he had on his plate, until she could take her first few wobbly steps on her own.

She set Laura's room right after Mr. Childers hired a cleaning team to erase the aftermath of the storm and the pointless mess of fingerprint dust. Once things looked just right, Charlotte took to falling asleep on the stiff, new mattress, holding one of Laura's T-shirts or county fair stuffed animals. Nothing in the room was changed.

She did get rid of Bubba Wallace, which didn't take much. Mr. Childers put him up at the motel, so he'd be out of her hair but within reach of the law. It was much easier for most to believe that Laura had run away than it was to believe something as horrible as an abduction, or worse, could happen in the tranquil town. So it fell upon her to press for information from the impassive authorities. But all she learned was that there wasn't much to glean, due to the law never thinking the case was anything more than a runaway kid. However, when Sheriff Reed was appointed, he allowed her to review the scant documentation the previous regime had gathered regarding the disappearance of her daughter. That was when she learned there were no threads to tug on, no leads to follow that might unravel the mystery of what happened to her only child.

It was difficult for her to believe that Bubba could have done something to hurt Laura. But then she learned about his criminal record, and possibilities spun through her restless mind mercilessly. Every moment filled with frantic uncertainty she could not turn away from. The not knowing was blinding, and suffocating, all-consuming.

As time moved on, she began to accept that Laura was gone forever. She had long since stopped going to town. She knew there were those who blamed her for Laura's disappearance, and she couldn't bear the judgmental glances. The sight of one of Laura's classmates as they grew up and moved beyond their place in Laura's world, when she knew her daughter could never do the same, was too much to digest, so she changed her ways and traveled an extra twenty minutes to the smaller, less familiar town of Perkins to do her shopping, get her hair done, do her banking, and tend to other errands.

Every street in Stillwater seemed too alive with memory, but she couldn't leave. She had to stay put, so Laura could come home to the place she loved, if by some small chance she were still alive. And here she could take care of the people who had taken care of her.

She beat herself up for her own role in the matter. A good mother wouldn't leave her child alone with a lowlife like Bubba. He always denied having laid a hand on Laura, but he'd been the one who allowed her to slip through the window either by her own device or with someone who intended to harm her.

When she started having visions of Laura standing out in the fields on the ranch, she knew her baby was gone from this earth. She understood these weren't figments of her tormented mind; this was a visitant. Her daughter was reaching out to her. But knowing her child was gone forever, and accepting that truth, especially in the absence of proof, was an almost impossible assertion.

At no time during the punishing pain had she ever considered giving up on her own life to end the unrelenting ache. Maybe she deserved all the suffering for allowing harm to come to her baby. She pleaded with herself for forgiveness that would never come. Although she doubted her capabilities, she did her best to give as much as she could to those who needed her.

THIRTY-FOUR

Two years after Laura went missing, Miss B passed. Her steady decline was lovingly managed by Charlotte, who had plenty of hours to care for her as she neared the moment of her last breath. It happened one evening when the setting sun reached through the window in the sunroom and touched Miss B's face. Charlotte was there, as was Mr. Childers and their son Thomas. Charlotte quietly hummed Miss B's favorite songs as she left behind the confusion and turmoil that marred her final years.

Charlotte was there for Mr. Childers in all that followed, and he was there for her. There was never the fear that she would have to leave the trailer, and even when she cut her hours at The Roadside, he never lowered her pay.

She found him one morning under the MossyCup Oak. His new collie, Mavis, was feverishly barking while refusing to leave her fallen master's side. His heart had given out just as he set out to cross the fields and check in with the ranch hands. Charlotte knew there was no better place for the man to lay down his life.

Even with all he had given her in his living years, she was astonished by how much he continued to care for her after he left. In his will, he shared everything with her, a fifty-fifty split with his son, Thomas. She got the trailer, some land, his prize mare, and a barn. All the things she used to think she wanted in life before she learned of true longing. He left her the motel, which she quickly sold off to the Watts family in a deal her lawyer called a steal.

Thomas moved into the ranch house while she tended to the matter of all the loose ends. He was dealing with more than the loss of his father, as he'd also lost his wife to his partner at his law practice. There was no way he could stay in business with the man who now lived the life he had once shared with his wife and sons. He decided to start over, and opened a small practice near the Payne County Courthouse. The worst part was the time he had lost with his boys, only seeing them for holidays and summers.

He and Charlotte grew close as she showed him the tempo of the ranch, and they picked through the treasures of Wallace and Betty Mae's lives. The two had almost grown up together, and this union felt comfortable and consoling, easy and right. His love couldn't fill the void left by Laura's absence, but he was good to her, and she felt almost whole again as she taught his boys how to ride, and how to care for their grandma's flower gardens, Mavis, and the chickens. In a sense, she was growing a family again.

The search for answers never ended. She worked tirelessly, demanding action from authorities, using the media to keep the story alive, since she knew things could turn as the players aged and relationships shifted. Hope lifted each time a news story ran—maybe it would be that whisper in someone's ear reminding them of something they saw or felt or heard. Maybe that voice would murmur annoyingly in their ear until they walked into the sheriff's office and offered up their hunch.

The methods used to keep the story in the forefront of people's minds changed as time passed. Once, all the details were repeated on television and in newspapers, and Laura's face had once been seen on cartons of milk at family tables. Now, her image was held in the hands of prisoners, on the backs of playing cards, and theories were shared and debated on blogs and websites. She scrolled through the online comments, always searching for one that might ring true, perhaps from a person who knew too much. Every lead that might hold water was carefully scrutinized until it evaporated.

Life at the Dark Horse Ranch continued with so many of its originators gone now. Thomas and Charlotte wed. They held a small ceremony under the Mossycup Oak, a tree that now symbolized the loss of two young souls. Even after the passing of Mr. Childers under the very same tree, Charlotte still believed the oak was a monument to hope and love and life. The tree had seen so much sadness, so much happiness, so much change. Yellow flowers were chosen to match the yellow bow as it remained tied around the tree's trunk that, on their wedding day, had added ten growth rings since Laura vanished.

THIRTY-FIVE

By 2020 Thomas and Charlotte had celebrated their silver anniversary and were living a quiet life on the ranch surrounded by a growing family. They were doting grandparents of three young girls. Both boys followed in the path of the men before them, Charles becoming a lawyer and Russell using his degrees in Computer Programming and Animal Science to develop smart ear tag technology for cattle, which would have made his grandfather proud.

In late March of that crazy year, Charlotte woke before sunup and rolled over in bed to find it empty. Thomas wasn't lying next to her. She was drenched in sweat and heat spilled out of her body. Her soaked nightgown turned icy hot as she sat up and saw the light escaping from the bathroom door which stood ajar, light cutting a wedge into the darkened room. A deep cough emitted from beyond the door.

She sat up too fast and was reeled by a wave of dizziness. "Thomas?" Her voice was a whisper, her throat sore and dry. As she rose from the bed, every joint in her body moaned in disagreement. Her whole body hurt. "You okay in there?" she questioned, standing on the other side of the door as his baying cough continued.

"Not feeling well at all, dear," he replied as he came to door. She could feel the heat radiate off him. Neither of them was willing to give voice to the potential that they had contracted the dreaded virus.

"Let's check your temperature," she said, pushing past him, reaching for the medicine cabinet. She spotted the thermometer and hoped it still worked, unable to remember the last time it was used. She grabbed cotton balls and rubbing alcohol and guided him to sit on the edge of the tub.

"Try to keep this under your tongue long enough for it to register, no coughing."

His fever was 102.2.

"Why don't you go back to bed? I've got some cold medicine in her somewhere. I'm going to need some myself," she said as she rummaged through the cabinet, and Thomas returned to bed. She cleaned the thermometer and placed it under her own tongue. Her temperature was 101.9.

She fought the urge to steal a gulp of tap water as she filled their counter cups and broke off two blister packs.

"As soon as Dr. Sawyer's office is open, I'll give them a call and see if they can squeeze us in today. For now, take these and let's see if we can get some sleep." She placed the water and medicine on Thomas' nightstand and returned to her side of the bed. The water burned her throat as she swallowed the gel caps, denying her relief from the searing pain she had hoped it would bring.

"Do you think we have the virus?" Thomas asked, addressing the elephant in the room.

"I can't imagine what else it could be. Maybe the flu?" she said. Trying to position herself in a way that eased some of the aching in her body and head, she said, "I felt fine going to bed, but now ..." She reached down to the end of the bed and pulled up the winter comforter that was neatly folded, close by in case of an early spring cold snap. The shivering came from within her body, and she couldn't calm the trembling.

Thomas tossed the blanket off himself. "I'm burning up," he mumbled before being overcome by another coughing fit. She greedily grabbed his discarded share and pulled it tightly under her chin. The medicine didn't touch the headache, but somehow she drifted off.

A feverish haze clouded her mind, and as the next few hours passed, Charlotte wasn't sure if she was asleep or awake. She only knew discomfort, and was incapable of pinpointing which part of her hurt worse. Her body fought more intense chills as she came to. Her pajamas clung to her. At some point in her delirium, she had thrown the blankets onto Thomas, who had hungrily gathered them around himself. Their bed trembled with the force of the chills their bodies were powerless against. Beside her, Thomas's cough had worsened; his breathing was rough and unsteady.

The room spun and vertigo grabbed her and swung her in its grasp, as she forced herself to contact the doctor. They were turned away, told to go to the emergency room. That didn't sound right to her, but she sensed Thomas needed medical care worse than she did. He was never one to be dragged down by a bug. She needed someone to assure her things were going to be okay.

Russell drove them both to the hospital, a bandanna tightly wrapped around his face and all the windows rolled down. They refused his help in taking the few steps to his car and once again to the hospital entrance, despite their difficulties walking on their own. They clung to each other for support, unsure if they were helping or hindering. Her fear mounted as the certainty became clear. She had never been so sick in her life.

Stillwater Medical Center met the needs of much of Payne County, and was learning along with the rest of the world how to help those who were infected. A CT scan indicated that Charlotte and Thomas did indeed have the virus. She had been right about Thomas—his condition was worse than hers. A nurse informed them that the virus oftentimes hit men harder. Charlotte was sent home with a remedy for all the possibilities and a pamphlet telling her what to watch for, the signs that might tell her to head back to the hospital. Thomas was admitted, but never to ICU, so he avoided a respirator.

Time stood still for Charlotte, back home, alone. Megan, Russell's wife, made soups and teas for her. Russell dropped them off on the front porch, texting Charlotte to get the items quickly, before they got cold. She did as she was told and all the things she knew she should. All the carefully made potions would help her, even if she couldn't describe their taste or smell. Russell temporarily moved into the old trailer where she and Laura had lived, isolating from his wife and baby. Megan took care of little Manda all alone for sixteen days, a little longer than the recommendations, just to be sure.

As it turned out, the virus might have saved Charlotte's life. One day the phone rang, and she was sure it was Dr. Sawyer's office calling to checking to see how she was fairing. Instead, she learned that her CT scan showed the shattered glass appearance the virus imprinted on her lungs, but upon review, something else suspicious was noted. A re-scan was suggested. The doctor assured her that it was prudent to rule the spot out as a possible test error.

It was no defect of the test. Something was there, a small spot that didn't belong. The good news was that the timing couldn't be better, and it had been caught early. The bad news was that it was likely cancer. Her doctors wanted to act fast, but warned about the unknowns of what surgery might to do to virus-weakened lungs.

Thomas tried to prepare her for how insufferable being alone in the hospital would be. He described the intimidating fear and anxiety of being cared for by faceless beings who had once been unique, individual doctors and nurses but were now hidden behind layers of PPE, robbing them of their ability to connect with their patients. He was unable to convey how best to ready herself mentally for the loneliness of the traumatic stay. There were far too many emotions from one minute to the next as the frantic beeping of machines never ceased and isolation took hold. Each piece of miraculous equipment sang a mournful song of those whose own voices were silenced by oxygen masks, or worse yet, tubes that breathed for them.

What she remembered most about her experience, alone after part of her lung was removed and she fought to regain her strength and breath, were the dreams. Every moment her eyes were closed, she was dreaming. It was always the same dream, of Laura standing just outside her reach, boasting, "I've worked so hard, Momma. It's finally going to happen."

"Who's Laura?" a nurse asked one day. "You say her name while you're sleeping."

Even when she was back home and didn't have untold medicines coursing through her veins, the dream kept on. She could no longer believe their realness was drug-induced. Laura was trying to tell her something. Perhaps that was why she wasn't too surprised to see the sheriff's car rolling up to the ranch house, kicking up gravel dust in its wake. Something was about to happen, just as Laura had promised.

THIRTY-SIX

Sheriff Doug Rayne and Pastor Elliot were shrouded in solemnity as they donned their face masks and approached the Childers' door. Charlotte was sitting in the living room doing her breathing exercises. Even though the view wasn't as nice as the sweeping view from the sunroom, she had never taken to the room where Miss B spent most of her last years. It was remodeled after Miss B's passing, its clinical appearance having been erased long ago, but it still held Miss B's ghosts. As Charlotte rose to welcome her unwanted guests, she knew this room was about to become inhabited by ghosts of its own.

"Thomas!" Her first attempt came out as a raspy, rough whisper. She found strength and volume on her next try. "Thomas!" she yelled, slowly walking toward the door on unsteady feet.

Thomas rushed into the room, fearing she'd fallen, or just fearing. The dish towel he held dropped from his hand, left forgotten as he rushed to her side to open the door to news that would be life-changing.

"Mr. and Mrs. Childers," Sheriff Rayne said, nodding as he removed his large hat.

"Come in, please," Charlotte said politely, opening the door fully, stretching out a hand. She wondered how she found manners and grace in this moment. She had envisioned this event countless times, and this was never the way she believed she might react.

"Sheriff, Pastor, have a seat. Can I get you something? I just took the kettle off the stove, tea maybe, or water?" Thomas rambled, and she was grateful he was taking the lead. He wrapped his arms around her and guided her to the sofa, helping her sit.

"No, sir. Thank you, though," Sheriff Rayne replied. He and the pastor sat across the coffee table in a pair of high-back chairs.

"I wish I could offer an embrace, Charlotte," Pastor Elliott said.

Charlotte nodded her head, giving the impression, she hoped, that she understood what he was saying.

The sheriff put an end to the awkward moment by saying, "We believe we've found Laura."

The air left her battered lungs in a rush. Thomas reached for the oxygen tank she had been sent home with. She hadn't been forced to use it yet, but he had practiced with the knobs and familiarized himself, so he wouldn't be left fumbling in an emergency.

Charlotte took the oxygen mask without thinking about it and held it to her face, forcing herself to breathe slowly.

Sheriff Rayne and the pastor sat in practiced silence.

A million questions rushed into her mind and clamored for attention as she tried to process what little he had told her. Each burning demand held no hope that Laura might be alive, but after all this time the chance for some resolution over-whelmed her.

"Go on, please," is all she could say.

Taking a folder out that he had tucked under his arm, the sheriff said, "I have some photos of the items recovered with the remains. While we are awaiting confirmation from the coroner, I do believe the articles strongly suggest the remains are those of Laura. If you are up to it, I can show you."

The sheriff was looking at Thomas as he spoke, and Charlotte now looked to him too. She was lost, but couldn't keep her eyes off the folder as it was passed across the table.

"The first photo is a picture of the items we found, the most telling one being the watch. There are some pieces of fabric and a pair of rubber boots, all consistent with what you described."

Charlotte took the folder from Thomas and handed it back to the sheriff unopened. "It's my girl," she said. "That's my Laura. I don't need pictures to tell me." She sat numbly and listened to the few details. Laura had likely died the very night she went missing, if not soon after, and so close to home. How could she have been so nearby this whole time?

"We hope to know more pending the autopsy report." He slid his card across the table, and Pastor Elliott led them in a prayer before they rose to leave. There were no departing hand-shakes, no hugs of condolence.

Charlotte sat in the same spot for hours after they left. Thomas tried to get her to eat. He tried to get her to talk. She could do nothing, so he sat beside her in silence until he felt her body weigh heavier on his. Then he gave her a gentle nudge, helped her up and put her in bed. Thomas tenderly eased her back to the pillows, covered her up, lay down next to her, and they slept.

Over the next few days, the only time she spoke was to ask Thomas if he would drive her to the place where Laura had been all these years. He would not do that to her. Russell had already warned him that the town was overrun by media trucks from Tulsa and Oklahoma City. People were looking for any news that didn't relate to the pandemic, so the story had become even more popular.

Sheriff Rayne met with them virtually to share more information. Numbness cloaked her again as he relayed additional facts.

"While the autopsy couldn't pinpoint the exact time of death, we interviewed several people. Mr. Harold Buhl remembered the time very well. He was the contractor who dug the pool. His wife kept meticulous records which made connecting the dots easier. He has been ruled out as a suspect," the sheriff told them.

"There was blunt force trauma to the skull, which is believed to have contributed to her death. Unfortunately, due to the advanced state of decay, there are still questions. But there is nothing indicative of bullet or stab wounds. The depth and makeup of the soil provided a somewhat preservative environment, allowing us to rule out strangulation. There just isn't enough to go on to know exactly what happened. The only anomalies are the skull fracture and her boots being on the wrong feet. Have you ever read an autopsy report, Mrs. Childers?"

She shook her head, unable to find words.

"I'm sending the file in an email. It might be best for you to go over it first, Mr. Childers. These things can be unbearable and confusing," the sheriff advised.

"Thank you, Sheriff. We'll take that into consideration," Thomas said.

"Do you think she was murdered, Sheriff? Did Bubba kill

my baby?" She almost yelled the words as the two biggest questions she had jumped to the front of her mind.

"I'm sorry, Charlotte, I wish I could answer those questions," he replied. Seeing her reaction, he continued, "Were you aware that Bubba's been locked up down in Texas since 1990?"

"No, I wasn't. What'd he do?" she asked desperately while holding her breath. If he had done something to harm a child, she wouldn't know what to do with herself.

"Seems he got himself in with a burglary ring. He was driving the getaway vehicle one night when things went wrong inside the house his partners were working over. The homeowner was shot, almost didn't make it. Bubba got a pretty stiff sentence. He should have gotten out a while back, but he hasn't exactly been a model inmate. His temper got the best of him, and he stabbed his cellmate. That sealed his fate with the Texas Parole Board."

He spoke of a man Charlotte didn't know. But had her daughter known him? If she had, Charlotte felt she was to blame.

"I tried to contact him to see if he had anything to say for himself in light of these discoveries. He'd filed for an emergency release due to the pandemic; compassionate release they're calling it," he said with a scoff. "Bubba's paperwork wasn't processed in time. After I got through the red tape and arranged to speak to him, I was informed he'd fallen ill. Tested positive. When I checked back a week later, he'd died. The virus got to him before I could."

Charlotte could see the sincere disappointment in the man's face. She wanted to tell him he probably wouldn't have confessed to killing her if he had, but she wasn't sure that was true and couldn't bring herself to comfort someone while she was hurting so badly.

"No one claimed his belongings, so I asked for them to be

sent to me. Maybe there's something there that will tell us more. It's a long shot, but I don't want to leave anything unchecked. I'm sorry to put all this on you at once, Charlotte."

Charlotte couldn't find her voice, but Thomas spoke. "Thank you, Sheriff. It is a lot to take in. Please let us know if you learn anything new."

The two men finished the call like people who weren't processing thirty-six years of devastation in a matter of minutes. She shut down again and Thomas took care of her.

THIRTY-SEVEN

Dad was having a hard time believing he had just taken a call from the actual Mayor of Stillwater, but he was having an even harder time believing he was looking at a very official check in the absurd amount of fifty-thousand dollars. It was made out to none other than Maxwell and Carin Weizak. It was the reward for information leading to the recovery of Laura Combs, and he had signed for it earlier that morning.

It had never occurred to him that they might be presented with the reward fund. None of it seemed real anymore. Receiving the phone call and the check had occurred within hours of each other. Mayor Wills asked him if his family would like to attend Laura's service.

Mom insisted that they couldn't keep the money. It wasn't right. She was just starting to believe that they could put this all behind them, and maybe remodel the house and learn to love it again. They all agreed that changing the exterior of the home would take priority, hoping that it wouldn't forever be recognized as the house in the news reports.

Holden and Hazel didn't learn about the windfall until

after the decision had been reached to donate the money to a charity chosen by Charlotte Combs-Childers. Emotions were high still, but the twins had recently learned that a decision about their first year at Stillwater High School was also made without their input. They tried not to focus on the knowledge that they would be doing distance learning, again.

There was a calm in the house. No longer were any of them struggling with the unknown, or the tightly coiled tension that left them doubting themselves constantly. Hazel was able to sleep again and tried to soak in the rest of the summer while still wondering how the remainder of her high school days would play out. She longed for life to return to normal.

Dad would joke, "Your generation will have the best 'back in my day' stories to come along in a long time."

To which she would reply, "Too soon, Dad. Too soon."

THIRTY-EIGHT

The morning of Laura's homecoming was calm and sunny, but cool. The hot, oppressive days had come to an end, just in time for most Oklahomans to doubt their ability to take another day of hot weather and suffocating humidity. It was that tenuous time when most were hopeful that the cooler temperatures would stay for a while. Fall in Camelot Crossing was breathtaking. The leaves were beginning to turn, painting colorful reflections off the ponds that dotted the neighborhood. Shades of green surrendered to a myriad of orange, red and yellow. Still, summer would be missed by most, even a summer as ridden with strife as 2020.

Sparkling dew clung to webs along the tree-lined streets of Sheffield Court and Range Road, betraying their weaver's normally hidden art as the Weizaks made their way to Laura's funeral. All of them tugged on waistbands and collars and shifted in their too-tight shoes as they made their way into town.

Mom wondered out loud, "How did I wear this stuff every day? It feels so weird."

A line of cars wrapped around The City of Stillwater Community Center when the Weizaks arrived to follow the procession to the cemetery. The stately building had been the junior high the last year Laura attended school. The Weizaks sat in silence waiting for the escort to begin the slow crawl down Main Street and 6th Avenue to the place Laura would be laid to rest. Groups of people lined the streets in clusters and traffic pulled to the sides of the roads as the procession snaked its way through town. Some bystanders were crying, holding signs with messages of homecoming and grief.

Before Charlotte and Thomas had left the ranch that morning, Charlotte had quietly taken a pair of scissors to the yellow ribbon that circled the Mossycup Oak. She held the faded bow as she sat in the swing and cried before walking to the trailer and placing it on Laura's bed. Now from the limousine that traveled in the shadow of the hearse, she tried her best to read all the signs. The outpouring of community was still fashionable in the small town.

Charlotte searched the masked faces, struggling to recognize the mourners as they exited their cars at the grave site. Time often made familiar faces more vague, but the masks made them almost ambiguous.

Their heads lowered in mourning, the guests were directed to clusters of chairs that matched their carload's number of occupants. The seats were too far apart for any to speak to others. A camera was set up near the grave site to live stream the funeral, allowing the town to watch. Charlotte believed she picked out the Weizaks the moment they passed by her. She found herself fixated on the family, wishing she could speak to them but having no idea what she would say if she could.

Thomas read the words that Charlotte wrote. She was unsure of her voice and didn't want to break down. It was important to her that her words were heard by all. He did her tribute justice as he spoke of Laura's love of animals and music and reading, as well as her beauty, kindness and sweet disposition. Thomas told his own stories of Laura, of her days as a youngster on the ranch.

The Weizaks sat in stunned silence as Thomas spoke of Laura's pet cemetery. Mom squeezed Dad's hand as he described how Laura lovingly cared for the barn cats in life and in death.

Hazel closed her eyes as emotion crashed upon her. She felt as if she had known the girl, and now realized she would miss her despite the upheaval she had caused. Something tickled her hand and when she opened her eyes, she found two ladybugs had landed—one on her hand and one on the face smiling at her from the front of the memorial pamphlet. Not a loveliness, but enough to assure her that a part of Laura would always be with the Weizaks.

COMING SOON!

DEEP WATER

Shadows of Camelot Crossing

A Haunting in Stillwater

As Lula Clarkson lay dying in the dwindling days of 2020, her daughter Wren paid her a visit. Lula's youngest girl hadn't aged a minute since Lula had last seen her that bitter winter day ten years past. Wren held in her arms a bundle of pink blankets and swayed gently in the corner of Lula's dark bedroom. No words were spoken. It was just a quiet visitation to convey goodbye, or perhaps, hello.

ACKNOWLEDGMENTS

Thank you to my family for supporting me and my dream; my friends for cheering me on, and an amazing team of editors who helped me make this happen.

ABOUT THE AUTHOR

Lisa Courtaway lives in Stillwater, Oklahoma and is married with four children. An entourage of four dogs and two cats follow her everywhere. She has worn many career-hats, from advertising to insurance to education. But her most rewarding title was Medical Paraprofessional to a fabulous bunch of kids at a middle school in Littleton, Colorado.

She loves a good ghost story, and has lived in several homes that spoke to her in mysterious ways. True crime stories, watching a binge-worthy series, reading, and taking care of her family are her favorites.

Since she was young, people have often told her she should write a book ... so she did.

You can find out more about Lisa, including her social media links, at her website www.lisacourtaway.com